The Pearl in the Attic

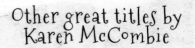
Other great titles by
Karen McCombie

The Year of Big Dreams

Life According to . . .
Alice B. Lovely

Six Words and a Wish

The Raspberry Rules

The Ally's World series

The Girl Who Wasn't There

Catching Falling Stars

The Whispers of
Wilderwood Hall

The Pearl in the Attic

Karen McCombie

SCHOLASTIC

Scholastic Children's Books
An imprint of Scholastic Ltd
Euston House, 24 Eversholt Street, London, NW1 1DB, UK
Registered office: Westfield Road, Southam, Warwickshire, CV47 0RA
SCHOLASTIC and associated logos are trademarks and/or
registered trademarks of Scholastic Inc.

First published in the UK by Scholastic Ltd, 2017

Text copyright © Karen McCombie, 2017

The right of Karen McCombie to be identified
as the author of this work has been asserted by her.

ISBN 978 1407 16410 6

A CIP catalogue record for this book
is available from the British Library.

Printed by CPI Group (UK) Ltd, Croydon, CR0 4YY
Papers used by Scholastic Children's Books are made
from wood grown in sustainable forests.

1 3 5 7 9 10 8 6 4 2

www.scholastic.co.uk

*For Kate and Penny, who can see
Ally Pally from their own attic...*

Prologue

Hornsey, North London, 1947

Tom slammed the door of the attic, ran over to the iron bedstead and punched his pillow till feathers puffed clean out of it.

His mother would be cross about the burst pillow, of course, but it was better than taking his rage out where it was due.

Oh, yes; his little brothers had done it again.

Destroyed something precious.

Last month one of them had broken a wing off his prized RAF bomber plane, and neither of them had owned up to it. On Tuesday, he'd found them posting his brand-new Subbuteo football players down the big cracks between the floorboards in the stockroom at the back of the shop.

1

But today . . . today they had damaged something old Auntie Gertrude had trusted Tom with.

He was so angry with himself; when he took the folded package of papers home from her house, tied so neatly with red ribbon, Tom knew he should've come straight up to the flat and read the story here in the quiet and calm at the top of the house.

Instead, he'd gone along the alleyway at the side of the shop, and into the yard. His father would be busy in the bakery at the back there as usual, but Dad always liked to hear news of Grandad Will and Granny Mary, and old Auntie Gertrude too, after Tom had taken them round a fresh loaf and a bag of scones for their afternoon tea.

But the twins were in the yard, roaring and jumping in puddles, not caring if they risked Mum coming out of the back door of the shop and telling them off for ruining their shoes and muddying their socks.

Maybe it was the fact that they were already so grubby that they were more aware of the yellowed but tidy folds of paper in their big brother's hand.

Before he knew it, Tom was ambushed, one twin crashing into him and pinning his arms, the other grabbing the story right out of his hands.

"Whee!" the twins had yelled, running around like imps, throwing the ribbon-wrapped package from one to the other, till the scarlet bow unravelled and the pages fluttered like dying butterflies into the muddy puddles of the bare yard.

When Tom began yelling – *swearing* at them, even – the boys started up with their usual sobs, realizing, too late as always, that they'd behaved badly.

"Tom! Language!" Mum had said, appearing at the back door, having heard the commotion from the shop.

"They're only little, Tom," said his dad, coming to the doorway of the bakery and wiping his hands on a towel. "What was so important about a few bits of paper anyway, lad?"

Tom didn't stop to explain.

He ran back out into the alleyway, around the plate-glass window of the shop, and in through the front door that would lead him to the flat above.

Now – with a few white feathers twirling gently, like delicate parachutes, on to the bedside rug – Tom's anger began to ebb, and remorse took over.

He walked over to the little window in the sloped ceiling and pushed it open.

And there was his favourite view ... past the roofs and chimney pots of the buildings opposite, Alexandra Palace hunkered grandly on its hill, surveying all of Hornsey down below.

"How am I going to tell her?" he muttered to himself as he watched the dark dots of faraway birds dance and swoop about the glass domes and towers of the palace.

Tom winced as he remembered the hopeful expression on Auntie Gertrude's face as she took the package out of a drawer and handed it to him. A sweet scent of lavender had drifted out with it.

"Here's a little bit of ... well, *almost* family history, Tom," she said. "It's a sad story, but I think you're old enough to know it now. Come back tomorrow and we'll have a talk about it, eh?"

And tomorrow, he'd have to tell her he'd read nothing more than the first page – *For Aunt Gertrude, with love and regret, Ruby*, with a date of *28 August, 1928*.

Tom had peeked at that much of the story on the way home, but knowing how important it had seemed to Auntie Gertrude, he'd been determined to save the rest till he had peace to read it properly.

"Ha!" Tom laughed to himself wryly.

And then it came . . . an answering giggle.

He hadn't heard that for a while.

Like an echo from another room, he'd sometimes hear them: girls laughing softly, or chatting, sometimes a shush.

Tom had never been afraid.

The voices had come to him, just now and then, since he was small. They were only ever here, in the attic.

The faint trails of girlish sounds were a comfort when he was curled up in his bed, feeling ever so small and alone under the slanted ceiling, with only the sky and stars above it.

Another giggle and another, so faint that they might be carried on the wind. . . Tom smiled, his shoulders relaxing.

It was as if his attic companions were letting him know he was all right, they were all right, everything would be all right.

Taking a deep breath in, Tom knew what to do. He'd run back downstairs and see if he could salvage any of the soggy pages of the story.

And he'd ask Dad to bake the best cake that rationing would allow, to take to Auntie Gertrude tomorrow. . .

Family #fail

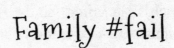

Chelmsford, Essex, 2017

I feel like throwing my stupid homework out of the living room window.

Wouldn't that be great?

Wheee!

Bye-bye, so long, got better things to do.

How delicious would it be to watch it soar through the air and end up three floors down in the car park of our block of flats? Even better if someone reversed their car over it!

But I guess I'd better not throw my homework anywhere, since it's online, and – more importantly – on Mum's work laptop.

CHUCK! *crunch*

Still, how am I meant to actually DO this assignment?

I stare again at the Show My Homework App on-screen. . .

Scarlet Sita Jones: Class 8E

Spanish: set by Miss Kendrick

Write about your extended family: Who are they? What are they like? Where and when do you see them?

OK, OK, I get it. Miss Kendrick expects a ton of Spanish vocabulary around the subject: stuff about swimming with cousins on seaside holidays; visiting aunties and uncles who always "Ooh!" over how much you've grown; grandads who try to teach you how to do magic tricks or tell you corny jokes or ask if you've got yourself a boyfriend yet. All the usual, normal whatevers.

The thing is, I can't come up with all the usual, normal whatevers.

Being the only child of an only child pretty much limits the whole extended family thing, especially if you have a gran you barely see and an invisible grandad on the other side of the world. As for my so-called father – don't even go there.

So yep, there's just Mum and me, me and Mum.

And even *we* don't have that much in common.

How do you say "My family sucks at being a family" in Spanish?

Hurray for Google Translate...

I quickly type in the sentence and get *Mi familia apesta a ser una familia* in return.

Copy.

Paste.

Press DONE.

Sorry, Miss Kendrick. I know it probably doesn't remotely mean what I want it to mean, but that's the best I can do.

So what now – watch something on Netflix? Or see if Bella or Aisha is around on Snapchat or Instagram? Yeah, one or the other, or both at the same time – *after* I get myself a snack. I'm starving, there's a leftover slab of M&S chocolate-and-vanilla cheesecake in the fridge, and tea (a ready meal I heated up about five seconds after I got home from school) was forever ago.

But uh-oh ... can I bear to go into the kitchen right now? Mum's friend Nicki is round. I can hear her through the wall. Her shrieky voice is just a high-pitched blur, but I can more or less guess what she's saying to Mum, since everything is always a look-at-me boast: "Did I tell you about the new four-wheel drive we're getting, Ren?"; "Hey, Ren, guess what – Bill's whisking me off to Paris, without the kids!"; "No word of a lie, Ren, Conor's teacher said he's like some kind of maths *genius*."

How Mum puts up with it I'll never know. Though she says my friends Bella and Aisha are as bad, even if their boasts are more about how many followers they have on Instagram or how many zillion Primark vouchers they got on their birthdays.

Thinking of my friends gives me an idea; I grab the home phone from its dock and press it to my ear. The dead burr of no connection hums in my ear.

"Yeah, sure, Bella . . . uh-huh. . ." I mumble into the mouthpiece as I head out of the living room, cross the box-sized hall and walk into the glare of the all-white, too-bright tiny kitchen. "Really? Wow. . ."

Nicki, with her mane of expensively dyed blonde hair, has her back to me. Mum is sitting on the other side of the just-big-enough-for-two table, still wearing her smartest pale-grey suit, since Nicki turned up with a bottle of wine and her list of boasts before Mum had a chance to change. You know, it always amazes me how my mother can look as pristine and groomed at the end of the day as she does at the beginning; her dark brown bob is glass-smooth, her make-up photo-shoot perfect.

And now she glances up at me with her kohl-

9

edged cat eyes, giving me that certain laser look she's so expert at. Its meaning is pretty interchangeable; sometimes she aims it my way when I've told her I've done all my homework ("*Really*, Scarlet?"), or sometimes it's like a secret, silent "Don't even *think* about it" (like when I asked for a two-week advance on my pocket money and Mum somehow *knew* it was for a crop top she wouldn't approve of).

It's silly, but I can't figure out the meaning of the stare straightaway, and for a second or two, I sort of feel as if the psychic message she's beaming might be, "Help . . . rescue me from this bore-a-thon, Scarlet!"

But nah; like I say, Mum and me aren't matey mum-and-daughter types. You won't find us wandering arm-in-arm round shopping centres together, or snuggled on the sofa with nachos and a box set of *Gilmore Girls*, and we certainly don't end text conversations with *Xxx*.

In fact, Mum's probably just staring at me 'cause she's guessed that I'm *totally* faking the phone conversation so I can get in and out of the kitchen – and fridge – without doing more than giving Nicki a quick, preoccupied wave.

Well, it's working just fine; Nicki is wiggling her perfectly manicured fingernails back at me, and blasts a not-actually-interested-in-you-anyway smile in my direction. The only time Nicki properly paid attention to me recently was when I dyed my hair lilac. When I say "paid attention", of course I mean "burst out laughing".

"Mmm, that's what *I* said," I waffle off the top of my head as I open the fridge and grab the plate with the cheesecake. "Yeah? No way! I mean—"

BRRR-BRRR! BRRR-BRRR!

I nearly jump a metre in the air when the phone goes and RINGS on me, *right* when I'm mid-sentence in my pretend conversation. My whole face blushes a fiery pink in the glossy, reflective surface of the nearest kitchen cabinet door.

Fumbling madly, I press the button to accept the call. At the same time, I turn to see Mum's laser gaze on me, more narrowed and glowering than ever. Nicki hasn't even noticed that I've been caught out in a lie; she's too busy flicking through some eBay posts on her Samsung and is blathering on about bidding on something she probably doesn't need.

"Uh, hello?" I say to the real-life caller.

"Hello," a woman's voice answers. "Could I speak to a Ms Renuka Chaudhary, please?"

"Huh?"

11

I know that isn't a very mature, polite way to respond, but I'm kind of stunned.

Sure, that version of her name is on Mum's birth certificate, but to everyone, *always*, Mum is just Ren. *Ren Jones*; I can see it clearly now on the ID card on the lanyard Mum wears to work every day, the one that's now been deposited on the kitchen table beside a bowl of peanuts Mum hastily put out for her visitor.

"Scarlet?" Mum frowns impatiently at me, motioning me to get on with it and speak, or at least pass her the phone.

"Have I got the right number?" the woman's voice asks into the void of confusion.

"Er, sure," I mutter. "I'll just get her for you. . ."

I walk towards the little table and hand the phone over.

"Hello? Er, yes . . . that's me. What's this about?" Mum answers in her crisp, boss-lady voice.

As she listens to whatever is being said, her frown deepens and her eyes widen.

"What! You have GOT to be joking!" Mum barks, getting up and tip-tapping out of the room in her patent black loafers. "What on earth. . .?"

"Oof!" laughs Nicki as Mum disappears off into

the living room and closes the door behind her. "Sounds like someone at work has messed up!"

"Mmm ... maybe," I mutter, feeling sorry for whoever is on the end of the line.

Having Mum as a *mum* is intimidating enough. Having Mum as a boss must be as much fun as having a migraine every day. "You have GOT to be joking!" – along with the glower of doom – is one of her favourite tactics for making you feel as small and annoying as a nit.

But according to the clock on the kitchen wall, it's nearly half seven, so who'd still be at the office? And even if it *was* a work person, who would call my mum a name that's well past its sell-by date?

"Her team is all getting ready for that big conference next week, aren't they?" Nicki says, distractedly going back to the eBay pages she's been drooling over on her small screen.

"Yeah," I reply, thinking of the piles of work Mum's been taking home every night lately.

I don't know what the conference is about, but that's not saying much; I don't even know what Mum's job is exactly. We all had to talk about our parents' work during a citizenship class in Year 7, and everyone's eyes glazed over when I said she was a project manager for an online office innovation company. I swear even the teacher was yawning.

"So, Scarlet, what are you up to at half-term?" Nicki asks, though I'm not sure she cares very much what the answer will be.

I feel a little bubble of happiness at the thought of the holiday, though. One more day of school tomorrow and then nine glorious days of pyjama mornings and mooching with the girls in the afternoons. 'Cause of the conference, Mum will be stuck at work more than ever, so it'll be like I'm living on my own. Now I'm thirteen, Mum's finally given in and stopped signing me up for holiday clubs, and I plan on celebrating by living off a diet of cheesecake and Pringles and dancing around the flat to music that's ridiculously loud. Maybe I'll even leave dishes in the sink all day and drape clothes from the laundry basket all around the flat, just to see what it feels like to break my neat-freak mum's no-mess rules. (Yes, of COURSE I'd have a mad binge of tidying ten minutes before she got home...)

"I'm just going to take it easy," I tell Nicki, though I can see she's tuned out already – looks like she's typing in a bid on a disgusting giant yellow leather handbag. "You know, robbing the Crown Jewels or inventing a cure for cancer, or maybe climbing up the fire escape to the roof and setting off a truckload of fireworks . . . that sort of thing."

"Uh-huh," mumbles Nicki, uninterested and deaf to everything I've just said.

OK, time for me and the cheesecake to leave.

I'm still smiling at the idea of standing on the flat roof of our modern apartment block and waking up the whole of Chelmsford with an out-of-season fireworks display . . . but then my grin slips as Mum barges back into the kitchen.

She has the strangest expression on her face

I've literally *never* seen her look this way before.

My very-together, always-organized, impressively immaculate mother seems suddenly lost, like . . . well, like some scared little kid.

As a family, I know we're an #epicfail; as a mum-and-daughter unit, we're kind of lame. But she's all I've got, and seeing Mum lose it makes *me* lose it.

SMASH goes the plate, cheesecake splatterings and shards of china instantly coating the glaze-tiled floor.

CRACK! goes an unknown something in the safe little world of us. . .

Down the Rabbit Hole

"Come on, come on!" Mum mutters.

She's not talking to me; she's snarking impatiently at the thin air behind the glass where a helpful member of staff should be standing.

"I'm sure they'll come in a minute," I say, though I'm drumming all my fingers on the chipped blue plastic surface of the reception desk.

"Oh, dear!" says someone.

We both turn to see that a passing nurse has come to a concerned stop beside us. She is staring at the blood-spotted toilet paper that was roughly wrapped around my right hand and is now untidily unravelling. I'd forgotten it was still there. I'd grabbed it in a rush as I followed Mum out of the flat earlier.

"Are you looking for the accident and emergency department?" the nurse asks. "It's down on the lower ground floor…"

"No, no, I'm fine – it looks worse than it is!" I say quickly, unwinding the rest of the grotty paper and holding up my quickly healing hand as proof.

"Ah, let me guess," says the nurse, smiling as she peers at the tiny, raw, pink nicks on my fingers. "Been playing with a kitten?"

"No," I answer, though I can see why it might look like I've been target practice for a sharp-clawed little kitty. Not that my mum would ever agree to a pet, since they're "messy" and need too much looking after, in her opinion. "It was because of the cheesecake."

The nurse raises a questioning eyebrow at me.

But Mum leaps in before I get the chance to explain that the multiple weeny scratches were *actually* caused by me trying to scoop up the dropped slab of cheesecake from the kitchen floor – without thinking of the minuscule shards of broken plate hidden in the chocolate-and-vanilla mush.

"Long story," Mum replies briskly, grabbing my home-made bandage from me and shoving it in her pocket to dispose of later. "We're here to see my mother. She's had a fall."

After the shock of the phone call, Mum's snapped into Practical Mode, her default setting. Mind you, even though she was trying to hide it, on the way here it was pretty obvious that she was deep-down stressed; the whole hour-and-a-half car journey from Chelmsford to London, she was driving so fast I kept finding myself gripping tight to my seat in case our Ford Focus did a Chitty Chitty Bang Bang and took off.

"Ah, OK!" says the nurse. "Well, the receptionist should be with you in a second, but who is it you're looking for?"

"It's Patsy Jones," says Mum. "I was told that she's broken her arm."

"And a collarbone, and some ribs and a couple of fingers," I add, just to be exact.

"Jones ... Jones ... I don't recognize the name," says the nurse. "There was *one* lady who came in tonight with multiple fractures, but it wasn't a Miss or Mrs Jones."

"Maybe she gave her name as Patsy *Chaudhary*?" Mum suggests.

"Yes! Mrs Chaudhary!" the nurse says with a nod of recognition.

I glance at Mum and see that she's clenching her jaw tight. She's wondering why Nana is suddenly calling herself by her old, married name; Nana and my grandfather divorced, like, seriously, forty years ago or something, and she's used her single name of Jones ever since. As for Mum, she stayed a Chaudhary for a while longer, finally changing it to Jones too when she was a teenager – and when she had long since lost touch with her dad back in Australia.

"Can you take us to her?" Mum asks.

"Yes, of course!" says the nurse, heading towards some double doors with a sign saying *Ward 9* above them. "I'll let you chat with her while I look for the doctor – I know she wanted a word with you."

Mum's jaw tightens again. It was bad enough getting a phone call to say that Nana had fallen in her flat and had several broken bones; it was more worrying to be told that there were "complications" which would need to be talked over with a doctor when Mum arrived at the hospital.

"One thing to be aware of: your grandmother might seem a little groggy from the painkillers," the nurse cheerfully tells me in particular as she breezes past lots of cubicles with curtains drawn. "Here she is! Patsy – it's your family to see you!"

Oh.

My heart sinks and tears prickle.

Nana's face is so pale under her pinned swirl of white-blonde hair. Under her bright blue eyes are storm-cloud dark circles. She's not *that* old – not even seventy yet – but looks so much more frail than I remember, especially with her whole arm and hand in a clompy L-shaped plaster cast.

And I guess the fact that she's generally looking so frail makes my heart sink and tears prick *more* than the worry over her broken bones. When was the last time I saw her? It's got to be more than a year, I realize with a gulp. It was when she was packing up and getting ready to leave her old house in Southend for the big move to London, the day she and Mum had that awful fight.

And when was the last time I spoke to her on the phone? I can't even remember; Mum does her polite, clipped, fortnightly duty phone call to Nana from work, usually.

"Renuka!" Nana calls out to Mum, lifting her *non*-plastered hand weakly from the top of the crisp white hospital sheet. "Well, well, well ... you came, darling!"

Mum hurries over and takes Nana's good hand.

I can see her clenching her jaw again. She's worried *and* confused. Nana – like everyone, everywhere – calls her "Ren". The painkillers are making her fuzzy, of course.

Or could it be concussion?

I just remembered Mum mentioning that possibility in the car on the way here; if Nana's had a fall, she might have bashed her head too. It's probably what the doctor wants to talk to Mum about.

"Of course I came," says Mum, doing her best to sound matter-of-fact, as she settles herself on a plastic chair beside the bed. "So how are you? And what happened?"

Wow, my mum and nan look so different when you compare them this close. I don't mean the age difference or the fact that one is healthy and one is a bit broken; it's just Mum's precise chestnut bob and olive skin are so very different to Nana's ultra-pale colouring and trademark bird's-nest bun (I can see the glitter of jewelled clips dotted in the straggles and messy curls of her up-swept hair).

"Oh, you know me," Nana answers with a wan smile. "Clumsy old thing – fell off my snowboard halfway down the piste."

I blink for a moment, and then remember that Nana is pretty funny. I suppose I forgot, since it's been so long and everything. . .

"Uh-huh. So what *actually* happened?" Mum asks her, brushing aside the joke.

If being an Organizational Fiend was a real subject, Mum would have a master's degree in it.

If Humour was a GCSE, Mum would score 0.

Now it's Nana's turn to tear up.

"It's not his fault that I fell!" she bursts out with a choking sound in her voice at Mum's blunt question. "When he bashed into me, I just lost my balance. So you mustn't be cross with him."

"Cross with who? What do you mean? Did someone *push* you?!" Mum asks. Standing behind her, I see Mum's shoulders twitch a little at this twist in the conversation.

"No! Oh, no – Mr Spinks didn't *push* me. Like I say, I just—"

"Ms Chaudhary?" a voice interrupts. It belongs to a young woman wearing a white jacket over her shirt and trousers. She gazes expectantly at Mum, who gives a little nod in reply. "I'm Dr Marek. . . Could I have a word with you in private?"

As Mum disappears off behind the curtain, I

shyly move away from the bottom of the bed and take her place beside my grandmother.

"Sita?" says Nana, as if she's just noticed me for the first time. (Concussion, for *sure*, since she's using my middle name.)

"It's Scarlet, Nana." I smile at her, my tummy tying itself in knots at the sudden guilt I feel for not seeing her in so long. Though it's hardly my fault, since it's her and Mum who are the problem. Or at least the problem is that they wind each other up so much that being in the same room together for any length of time gets both their blood pressures soaring through the roof. And when Nana wouldn't listen to Mum and insisted on going ahead with her mad plans to sell up in seaside Southend and move to London . . . well, that's when it all went wonky. Or more wonky than ever.

"I didn't recognize you, sweetheart," Nana says softly. "What colour do you call that?"

As Nana speaks, she raises her good hand to stroke the messy, lilac-toned layers that hang down around my shoulders.

"It said *Violet Skies* on the bottle. It's called a mermaid shade," I tell her, keeping my gran up to date with the latest hair fashion.

"Well, I *love* it," Nana announces, sounding and looking a little more like her usual self.

"Thanks! Mum's not very keen," I tell her. "Neither are the teachers at school. And my friends hate it – they say it's too freaky!"

"How very boring of them – it's a triumph! Now, you've got the same light blonde hair as me," says Nana, forgetting hers is more white these days. "Do you think I'd suit a mermaid shade too?"

Maybe she's joking again, or maybe she's serious – she *is* Nana, after all, a woman who's never knowingly shied away from anything exciting, alternative or creative – i.e., all the traits of hers that drive Mum around the bend.

She was the art student who married young, emigrated to Australia, then *un*emigrated back to Britain with a little kid in tow. She was the single mother who dragged my reluctant mum-as-a-kid on shoestring camping and backpacking trips all over Europe. She was the newly retired art teacher who bought a gypsy caravan for the back garden of her house as a retirement present to herself and scandalized the neighbours.

Of *course* she can have lilac hair, same as me.

"Yeah, why not?" I say, then try and get the

conversation back on track. "So, Nana, what *did* happen with this Mr Spinks?"

Once again, Nana's face crumples into despair.

"Oh, Mr Spinks . . . I hope he's not hurt too! And he'll be so worried about me, Scarlet. Can you go check on him, sweetheart? I can't bear it if he thinks it's his fault, and you need to tell him I'm all right really. Will you?"

My head is fizzling. Who is Mr Spinks? A neighbour? A lodger? A polite burglar who broke into Nana's flat and introduced himself before he pushed her down the stairs?

"Well, I—"

"I mean, if it was *anyone's* fault it was J. K. Rowling's. Ha!"

"Huh?" I mumble, frowning at Nana.

She sees my furrowed forehead and that seems to bother her.

"Oh, Scarlet! I've made everything such a muddle and a mess and worried everyone, haven't I?" says Nana, getting herself properly upset.

"No, I'm sure you haven't," I tell her, reaching for a tissue from the box on the bedside cabinet.

"But, sweetheart, I don't know what *time* it is over there, and the people from the hospital might have woken Dean up," she says, her hands flapping in distress. "And Zephyr's only a baby! I don't want them disturbing his sleep!"

Oh, dear ... that concussion must have *really* rattled poor Nana's head, and made her thoughts as mushy as the cheesecake that's still squelched over the kitchen floor back home. It's kind of scaring me, to tell you the truth.

I mean, do Mr Spinks, Dean and Zephyr actually *exist*? Or are they characters in some soap Nana was watching right before she tripped?

And what's J. K. Rowling got to do with anything?

"Oh, and before I forget, Scarlet," says Nana, a sudden sense of urgency in her voice as she dabs at her eyes, "you have to promise me something. It's important."

Nana fixes her cornflower eyes on me. They suddenly seem so softly vivid, like the *Washed-Up Mermaid* blue shade in the hair-colour range I use.

"OK..." I say warily.

"Listen, I don't want *anyone* but you to find the pearl in the attic. Do you hear me, Scarlet? It's just for you."

Outside the curtain, voices draw near, as Mum and the doctor finish their conversation – and I suddenly feel flooded with a sense of relief. I do love Nana, and I have missed her, but this conversation is taking a turn for the seriously weird.

"I hear you. Don't let *anyone* find the pearl in the attic, except me," I repeat. "Got it."

Of course I haven't got it.

All I've got is a thudding headache.

Compared to the last couple of hours, impossible Spanish homework seems as blissful as a week in Florida with a non-stop supply of free ice cream.

"Scarlet . . . here," says Mum, coming through the curtain, followed by the doctor. Mum's rifling in her bag, pulling some coins from her purse. "Can you grab me a coffee from the machine by the lift?"

I hesitate, suddenly irritated at Mum ordering me to run an errand, like I'm her PA or something.

"Oh, Scarlet," Nana pipes up. "Can you get a cup of tea for Angie while you're at it? She's always stealing mine."

This feels a bit like falling down the rabbit hole.

Everything is getting curiouser and curiouser.

"Sure," I say to Nana, grabbing the money from Mum and hurrying away from Wonderland/Ward 9 as fast as I can. . .

27

Keep Calm and Panic

Mr Spinks (who we mustn't blame for Nana's fall).

Dean (the snoozer).

Zephyr (the baby with the unlikely name).

Angie (the tea-stealer).

J. K. Rowling (the insanely famous author).

All the fanciful characters Nana made up or mentioned – turns out they weren't anything to do with the strong drugs she'd been given.

They weren't anything to do with bump-on-the-head fuzziness either.

She has dementia.

Well, probably. *That's* what Dr Marek wanted to discuss with Mum. Nana arrived with broken bones, but the doctor thinks there are fractures and fault lines in her mind too. . .

"I guess it explains why she had that ridiculous idea to move to *this* place," Mum mutters, as the car bleep-bleeps its locking system behind us. She sounds exhausted. We're both exhausted.

It's about ten p.m. and we're parked on Hornsey High Street in North London. It's not like the high street in our town; there's no Superdrug or Paperchase or Carphone Warehouse or whatever. Cars zoom up and down it, but it has a faded, forgotten feel.

Glancing either side as we cross the road, I see a kebab shop, a launderette, a small post office, a place selling second-hand furniture, a Tesco Express, an old-fashioned pub. Only the pub and the kebab shop are open, but they're hardly groaning with customers.

There are lots of empty, long-dead shops too, and that's what we're looking for: a derelict shop with a flat above it, a bell by the front door with JONES scribbled in the plastic-coated name section.

"I don't remember her being different, or seeming ill before she moved, though," I say, picturing Nana in her dungarees and stripy T-shirts, singing as she got on with her packing back at the house last year. That morning, before the big blow-up with Mum, Nana had me running around doing odd jobs for her: dropping off hand-painted goodbye-and-here's-my-new-address cards to her neighbours; making sure the bird feeders were all full; putting together a little posy of roses from the garden to welcome the new owners (I used a jam jar as a makeshift chunky vase – the jam jar Nana always kept her spare keys in, hidden under the hydrangea bush by the front door).

"Maybe it was just in the early stages then," says Mum. "Maybe we didn't notice because she's always been a bit. . ."

"Random?" I suggest.

"Exactly," Mum agrees with me.

"But out of anywhere she could move to, why did she want to come *here*?" I ask as I gaze around at this drab, uninspiring street.

"Well, I guess your nana *did* know this area already. When she left school, she came to London and studied art at a college somewhere around here," says Mum, telling me a bit of Nana's ancient history that I only hazily remember hearing before. "But honestly, Scarlet, when she said she was bored of being retired and wanted an adventure, I thought my mother was talking about trekking in Nepal for three months or something. I didn't expect it to mean packing up her whole life and moving to *this*."

Of course, *this* is what Mum has the problem with: Nana was originally from seasidey Southend, and when she and my mum returned from Australia, Nana headed back there, buying a ramshackle old house that she'd done up over time. Why – after all these years – would Nana want to leave a gorgeous house with sea views for some grotty flat above a shop on a busy, fume-filled road?

Thinking about it, I'm suddenly stabbed with a sharp twang of longing for that old house, even though I'd been going less and less, even *before* Nana moved away. Once I'd started secondary school, there were always shopping trips into town or plans to hang out with Bella and Aisha. You know how it is; if you don't go, you might not be asked again, or worse still, be talked about.

But when I was young, I was always super-excited when we were on our way to visit Nana... There was always fun stuff to do, either hanging out at the beach all day or just playing in her huge garden, which I *adored*, since we didn't have one our own in our modern block of flats. What would Nana have planned, I'd wonder. Would there be a paddling pool set up? Skittles made from a tennis ball and empty water bottles? A brand-new fairy door nestling in the tree roots? A paper-trail hunt, where the clues Nana had made up would be tied to pine cones, tucked under plant pots, hidden inside watering cans? A memory rushes in of me and Mum often having to let ourselves in with the hidden keys in the jam jar, if Nana was out of range of the doorbell, sketching or daydreaming in her caravan in the garden. . .

"Didn't Nana have some plan to buy a flat with a shop, that she could turn into a gallery?" I ask, the details now starting to drift back to me.

Nana's idea had been to open up a space for her own art, and other local artists, potters, sculptors, whatever. During the fortnightly duty phone calls, Mum had come to realize the gallery idea had never materialized, which didn't exactly come as a surprise.

"Mmm," mutters Mum. "Though how she thought she could start up a business at *her* age I don't know. And how was an art gallery ever going to work in a backwater street like this?"

As she talks, Mum holds up her phone, checking on the address Nana huffily gave her "for emergencies" a year ago. At the time, Mum vowed never to visit, and Nana vowed never to invite her.

Well, I guess it's an emergency now; at least, when the nurse gave us the keys to Nana's flat, Mum decided it was worth popping in on the way home to Chelmsford. Given the brace-yourself, *possible* diagnosis of dementia, the plan is to check that everything is locked up and safe – with no taps left running and causing a flood, or gas rings burning and setting off smoke alarms – before we head off on our long drive.

"So what's going to happen, Mum?" I ask as we walk.

I hug my arms around myself, suddenly feeling chilled to the bone, as if it's a frost-edged November night instead of a warm evening in late May.

But I guess that's what shock does for you. Shock at seeing your grandmother changed and poorly, shock at hearing that she has a creeping condition that wants to confuse and befuddle her and will steal her real memories and give her fake ones.

A condition, a disease that I don't know a whole lot about, apart from the fact that it doesn't go away.

Like some unchecked ivy, it's going to slowly curl around Nana's head till – eventually – she can't see out.

"I really don't know, Scarlet," says Mum, glancing around for door numbers in the gloomy light of the street lamps. "I've got that meeting at the hospital tomorrow, with a doctor on the neurological ward, as well as a social worker. That'll make things clearer. Till then, we shouldn't jump ahead of ourselves and assume the worst."

I know what Mum's doing: slipping into her Practical Mode. It's her way of keeping calm, keeping herself together. She's as rattled as I am, I know. I saw her quietly dabbing at her eyes when I came back to Nana's cubicle with the cups of coffee and tea earlier.

Anyway, if Mum's dealing with it like that, I figure it would help if I maybe acted the same way, so I take a deep breath and sound as practical as I can too.

"Do you think it might be *that* one?" I ask, pointing to the particularly dilapidated shopfront we're approaching.

"Possibly," says Mum, as we come to a stop on the pavement and turn to survey a patchwork of fly posters which completely cover a large plate-glass shop window. Even in the sickly yellow glow of the street lamp, it's plain to see the woodwork of the window and the shop door is rotten, with paint peeling in crackled curls and waves.

Directly above the window, some ancient, fastened-back awning seems to be trying to escape from where it's been concertinaed into its base; it dangles over a faded old sign for the shop, squeaking and swaying in the light breeze.

To the left of the shop is an equally rotten, paint-peeling tall gate in an arched entrance to an alleyway or passageway, I suppose.

"I guess *that's* the entrance to the flat upstairs," says Mum, taking a few steps towards a recessed doorway to the *right* of the shop. "Let's see what number it— Oh!!"

We both start in alarm, uncertain what the solid dark lump in the doorway *is* exactly.

But then I switch into Practical Mode a beat before Mum.

"It's just a bag of rubbish," I say confidently – then give a little shriek of alarm when I see that that the bin bag has two yellow eyes, and they're staring up at me.

So much for Practical Mode; it's just dissolved into a puddle of panic.

"It's a dog! It's just a dog, Scarlet!" Mum says, grabbing hold of my arm to settle me, and herself, I think. "Shoo! Go on! Shoo! We need to get in here."

We do – the number is right, and the bell on the door has JONES underneath, I see, as my thundering heart starts to settle.

The dog doesn't shoo.

It just carries on blinking up at us. The light is so dark in the shadowed recess and the dog is so black that I can't make out any features other than the yellow eyes. At least it's not showing sharp white teeth – yet.

Mum claps her hands together noisily to scare the dog away.

The dog stays where it is and keeps right on blinking up at us.

"Maybe it's lost?" I suggest, remembering how frantic Bella was last year when her pug slipped its collar and ran off in the park. Her family were so grateful when someone found Binky that they gave them a reward. "Let me see if it's got a collar and tag. . ."

"Careful," says Mum as I slowly kneel down. "It could bite!"

The dog doesn't bite. It just watches me warily, then begins to lick my hand as I reach out for its neck.

The tickle of its tongue makes me smile in spite of myself, in spite of the mood of this sad, strange, surreal evening.

"Yep, I can feel a tag. . ." I tell Mum, as my fingers fix on a cool disc of metal. "Can you get the torch app on your phone so I can read it?"

"Sure," says Mum, quickly flipping the light on and pointing it directly down.

The dog is almost completely round, with skinny little legs. I can see its face clearly now: the fur is black, but white with age around the muzzle, its eyes are more hazel-brown than yellow, one ear's a bit chewed.

It's a Staffie, I think, and properly funny-looking, borderline ugly even – which makes it kind of cute.

I melt a little bit.

However old it is, this dog is definitely giving me the pleading puppy look, like it's begging me for help.

I melt a bit more.

Dogs can sense things, and realizing it's got my attention, the Staffie raises a paw.

OK, I'm mush.

"Pleased to meet you," I say softly as I take hold of the offered paw with one hand.

With the other hand, I swizzle the dog's collar around to the left so I can read the disc properly.

When I see what it says, my stomach does a backflip.

"So, can you make out a phone number, Scarlet, or an address?" asks Mum.

"Yes," I answer, though it's the *name* on the disc that's grabbed my attention.

"Well?" Mum says impatiently.

"Mum, the dog ... it lives here," I reply, noticing now the lead that dangles down on to the worn doormat.

"*Here?*" Mum practically squeaks.

"Yep," I say, thinking that if she finds *that* hard to get her head around, wait till she hears what I've got to say next. "And it's called Mr Spinks."

At the sound of its name, the dog begins a whole-body waggle, its short tail smacking against the dusty front door.

"What? Nana has a *dog*...?" Mum says, again

with the high-pitched edge of surprise to her voice.

I turn and stare up at her. Once we'd left Nana's bedside and Mum talked me through the doctor's suspicions, I'd told Mum in turn about the nonsense Nana had come out with . . . the pearl hidden in the attic; the fantasy cast of characters.

In our current shared glance I can see we're both thinking the same thing.

What exactly is behind this door?

If Mr Spinks is real, what – or who – else is. . . ?

Knock, Knock, Who's There?

Mum wriggles the key in the stiff lock, and after a bit of a fight, it finally gives in and clunks open.

Mr Spinks is in before we are, his fat little body shooting like a bullet up what must be bare wooden stairs, from the clippetty-tappetting sound of his claws and the flip-flap of the bouncing lead.

"He must've got out when the ambulance men came to get Nana," I say as Mum scans the dark wall with her torch app for a light switch.

PING!

Success – the switch is flicked and the staircase ahead is illuminated with a huge white paper-lantern shade. It bounces in the breeze of the door opening.

At least I *think* there's a staircase there; it's hard to tell.

"You have GOT to be joking!" Mum mutters, standing stock-still, keys in hand as we both gaze open-mouthed at the teetering piles and heaps and *mounds* of books balanced on every step, leaning against both walls. There's a small, slightly twisting, book-free path up the middle between them, just wide enough for a pair of feet – or a small, fat dog – to get up and down.

A few scattered novels are spilled at the foot of the stairs, where Nana took her tumble. Mum was told that when the paramedics arrived – called by the owner of a nearby café – they'd found the door wide open and Nana crumpled and confused. She must've been going out or coming in from walking her dog, I suppose. Maybe she got tangled in Mr Spinks's lead. And I suppose he ran away due to all the chaos and kerfuffle of ambulance sirens and helping hands.

Hold on.

Harry Potter ... *those* are the tumbledown books, all early versions, by the look of the covers.

"Hey, Mum – is *this* why J. K. Rowling was to blame for Nana ending up in hospital?" I suggest. "She went and tripped over *The Prisoner of Azkaban*?!"

It would be pretty funny, if Nana wasn't in plaster . . . and the rest.

"Well, that makes some kind of sense, I suppose," says Mum, shutting the door as I try and quickly scoop the Potters back into a version of neatness. And going on up, I see that all the piles and heaps and mounds are loosely organized into genres: there are a bunch of gardening books, then a bundle of "How to Craft" type books here, little kids' picture books there, some that look like they might be detective stories from their covers . . . and on and on the stacks go, right up to a small landing at the top of the stairs.

"If this is out *here*, what on earth is it like inside?" I hear Mum mutter behind me.

What she says makes me glance up to the small landing ahead, where Mr Spinks is standing on his spindly hind legs, frantically scratching at a door.

A door that's painted sky blue with a giant grey parrot pictured in mid-flight.

"Do you think *Nana* did that?" I wonder aloud as I catch up with Mr Spinks.

It doesn't look too much like Nana's style . . . since she retired she's concentrated on painting endless views of the sea and the pier and the beach huts of Southend. Great, giant canvases of them. She was always putting on exhibitions in local cafés and craft shops and the library and wherever. Everyone seemed to love them; she sold bucketloads. But the only birds she ever painted before tended to be seagulls, not inhabitants of rainforests.

"I suppose so," says Mum, coming right up behind me. "What does the note say?"

I've been gawping at the impressive painting so much that I didn't take in the note that's pinned to the door frame. Nana's distinctive twirly, arty handwriting is instantly recognizable from a ton of birthday and Christmas cards she sent me and Mum over the years.

"It says: *'Please close the door behind you – think of Angie...'*"

As my voice fades away in surprise, I turn and exchange a quick glance with Mum.

So Angie is real too?

"Don't tell me it's another dog!" says Mum as she studies the note for herself.

"Maybe," I mumble, unsure, as I step back, hoping Mum'll go first.

She does; with a swift, deep breath she gingerly tries the handle.

But it seems Mr Spinks is *so* glad to be home after his accidental hours of exile outside that he's not bothering with doing *anything* gingerly. Instead, he headbutts the door wide open, and scuttles off into the darkness of the flat.

Mum's hand flaps at the wall just inside the door and *PING!*, another light pops into life. The pendulous shade overhead is an even bigger moon-shaped paper lantern, so big I'd struggle to wrap my arms around it.

So where are we? I *suppose* it's meant to be a hallway.

I mean, I can see three doors to rooms – as well as another staircase that must lead up to the next floor. It's just that getting to them won't be easy – not with the endless cardboard boxes to navigate.

Large boxes, medium-sized boxes, small boxes.

Plain boxes, Walkers Crisp boxes, shoeboxes.

They're like different-sized children's building blocks, balanced one on top of the other, with some of the stacks nearly reaching the ceiling and the paper moon above us.

"What do you suppose is *in* all of them?" says Mum, gazing up and around in horrified wonder.

"Um, according to that, it's assorted jigsaws," I say, pointing to a marker-pen message that's scribbled on the bottom box of the nearest stack. "The next one up says '*computer keyboards*', the one above that says '*old cameras*', and the shoebox on top … '*watches: broken but pretty*'."

"'*Rollerblades and skates*'; '*vintage handbags*'; '*Lego: assorted*'…" Mum reads from another batch of boxes, all the while shaking her head. "Oh, Scarlet; I had no idea your nana had turned into a hoarder! I mean, she always liked clutter and collecting things when I was growing up, but this…? Her dementia's made it get completely out of hand!"

Tink! Tinkle! Tink!

The small but distinct bell-like sound makes Mum and me freeze. It sends Mr Spinks into a spin, though, and we hear – even if we can't *see* – him whining and scratching at the closed door to the left. A light is on in the room beyond it; a sliver of brightness glints at the gap at the top.

"Hello?" Mum calls out. "Is someone there?"

"Hello?"

That simple reply, coming from the other side of the door, sends goose pimples coursing up and down my arms…

Nana's Secret World...

"Mum?" I whisper, hardly believing what I'm hearing. "Isn't that *Nana's* voice...?"

For just a second, I see that glimpse of the scared little girl in her eyes – and then Mum's fearless and unstoppable side kicks in again. With a careful wiggle she clears the box maze and reaches the door, turning the brass handle without a second thought.

But as soon as the door is flung open, something *hurls* itself out at us – spiralling and whirling in mid-air, with a terrible croaking and honking and flailing of sharp claws.

Mum and I are both screaming, Mr Spinks is howling, and I pray some neighbour through the wall hears our distress calls and comes to help us.

And then everything calms. . .

The flailing creature settles itself on the top of a box that once contained salt and vinegar crisps, tucks its grey feathered wings to its sides, and squawks, "Hello!"

OK, so this time the squawk is more like a voice. It's a perfect imitation of *Nana's* voice.

"A parrot!" Mum says, stating the obvious.

I have never come this close to a parrot, certainly not one that was spiralling and whirling horribly close to my head just a second ago, so I slowly begin edging between the boxes towards the safety of Mum, all the time keeping my eyes on the bird.

The bird keeps its beady eyes on me too.

Suddenly freaked, I bolt, bashing my shins on box edges, and hurtle through the open doorway.

But uh-oh . . . there's a scratching sound of claws leaving cardboard, and next thing I hear the thick flap of wings above my head.

"Aahhhhhhh!" I yell, and duck, certain I'll feel the sharp dig of talons in my scalp any second.

"Scarlet – shush, it's all right! It's OK! See?" says Mum, wrapping an arm around my shoulders and ushering me into the room.

It's a large room. A living room. At first glance I

can see it has three big windows on the wall that faces the street, two squashy sofas, one fat, floppy armchair, one white paper moon lightshade, about twenty old-fashioned phones with those funny circular dials in different shades arranged along a cabinet, about as many lamps (tasselly table ones, tall standing ones) dotted around, and too many stuffed black plastic rubbish bags to count, bundled on the floor, on the chairs, everywhere.

Panic and confusion keep my brain scrambled for another second, and then I see what Mum's pointing at, and what she means by everything being all right.

On the cushion-strewn armchair, Mr Spinks has settled himself down, a happy pink tongue lolling from his positively smiling doggy face.

Now come to rest on the small table next to the chair, the parrot bobs and ducks and tip-taps its clawed feet, all the while watching us nervously – till it pauses to put its beak in a mug and drink whatever's inside.

I recognize the mug; it says *World's Best Nan*. It's a gift I gave Nana one Christmas years ago, when I was about seven or eight. And I'm betting that there's tea in that mug AND that I can guess the parrot's name.

"Angie?" I say, testing out my theory.

"Hello!" Angie the tea-stealer replies, taking her beak out of the mug and flapping herself off the table at the sheer thrill of hearing her name. She lands on the top of a huge cage that's right behind the door, silver metal bells inside the cage *tinkle-inkle*-ing an echoing accompaniment to her excitement.

"Wow ... they're good, aren't they?" Mum says, staring now at the three huge paintings – canvases almost as tall as I am – on the back wall. They have a theme, these paintings: all of them feature a similarly sized circular shape, taking up nearly the whole of the canvas.

The one on the left is of a hot air balloon, ropes dangling below, in a bright blue sky.

The middle artwork is a luminous moon in a watery turquoise setting.

The one closest to us is of a big, circular window, a stained-glass window, in a red-brick arch set against a deep, inky indigo.

I wonder why Nana chose to paint those particular images?

"The pearl is beautiful," says Mum, pointing to the one in the middle, the one I thought was the moon. Of course it is; I can see that now ... there's no moon craters, just a smooth, cream-tinted sheeny globe.

At the mention of a pearl, I remind myself there are more rooms to explore in this madhouse – including the attic...

"Should we carry on looking around?" I ask Mum.

She shrugs a yes, as bamboozled as me, and we head off – accompanied by Mr Spinks and Angie as tour guides – to see what lies within the other two rooms on this floor.

First up is the kitchen (more boxes, more black bin liners, a crate of old teacups and saucers, toys and dolls packed eerily together on the dresser shelves), and then the bathroom (doing a great impression of being a normal bathroom, except for a laundry basket entirely filled with plastic yellow ducks).

Mr Spinks stops and stares up at us as we gawp around both rooms, wobbling from one front paw to the other as he tries to figure out who we are and what we might be doing here. Or maybe he's desperately wondering where Nana is and when she's coming back and is trying to use doggy telepathy to read our minds.

Angie is watching us closely too. She settles herself on the top of each door, head twitching, studying the strange, open-mouthed gasping creatures we are – and probably hoping one of us fancies filling up her seed bowl sometime soon.

"Ready to see upstairs?" Mum asks, taking a deep breath to prepare herself. Now it's *my* turn to shrug a yes. Of course I want to see more of Nana's secret world.

Once past the box forest of the hall landing, we wend our way up the next staircase, which this time is home to dozens and dozens of pair of shoes, from pointy, dainty, gold dancing shoes that perhaps belonged to a flapper girl of the early 1900s, to clompy silver platforms from the 1970s, to slouchy Ugg boots … all sitting neatly partnered on either side of each step. I can almost imagine an invisible presence standing in each pair, like a ghostly guard of honour, as we ascend.

And then a fat dog rushes past me, like an oversized black potato on cocktail-stick legs, and I can't help sniggering.

"Not quite so bad up here," says Mum, surveying the second-floor landing. "Though it smells pretty musty."

There are two clothes racks on wheels, both heaving with an assortment of old coats, dresses, shirts and skirts.

"Shall we try this one first?" I suggest, pointing to a room that's directly above the living room.

I lead the way in before Mum has a chance to answer. And we find ourselves in an art studio, with a desk virtually disappeared under sheaves of drawings on A3 sheets of paper and semi-finished vast canvases propped up on every wall. The floorboards are bare, and splattered with paint. Only the neatly made bed in the corner and the open book and alarm clock on the small table beside it give away the fact that this is also Nana's bedroom.

"How can she live like this?" Mum says quietly, almost to herself. "Maybe if I'd visited, I could have stopped it getting this bad. . ."

As she talks, she rests a hand on an empty easel and gazes at the view outside the three windows, which mirrors the ones downstairs.

The view consists of identical buildings opposite, though there's a decent amount of sky above the roofs and chimney pots, I suppose. But I'm turning to go already, 'cause I'm itching to see the last two rooms on this floor, and the attic too.

After all, we still haven't come across "Dean", baby "Zephyr" or the pearl that's meant for me and *only* me. . .

"C'mon," I say, heading back out into the hall, moving a wheelie rack of clothes out of the way and opening another door. "Whoa. . ."

"What? What is it?" asks Mum, hurrying after me when she hears my shocked gasp.

And then she sees what I see.

What this flat – so far – has not prepared us for.

We both gaze around the immaculate room, painted pale grey, with two single beds made up like it's some boutique hotel, with acid-yellow bedding and funky sixties-patterned cushions laid against the pillows. There's one painting on the wall, done by Nana of course, of a teenage boy on a surfboard, sandy-haired, in neon-green shorts, balanced on the crest of a white-tipped, azure-blue wave.

"I don't get it," says Mum. "Why is this room like, well, *this*?"

But I'm not listening; I'm hurrying through to the next room, moving another rail of clothes – which Angie is happily roosting on – to get to the handle.

"This one's just as neat!" I call out. "Neater, even!"

It's like Mum Heaven.

White walls blend with white draped curtains matched with a crisp white duvet on a double bed. An old dressing table with three mirrors has been painted white, for a shabby-chic effect. A white stool sits at it, painted white too, and with a pretty, rose-patterned seat of Cath Kidston fabric.

Again, there's only one large painting on the wall, this time of a single velvety red rose, so vivid I can practically smell the scent. That's Mum's favourite flower; whenever she's in a good mood, she'll come home with a bunch for the living room. Though she prefers to call them "scarlet", rather than red. And her love of scarlet roses was the inspiration for my name.

Scarlet for the roses, Sita because Nana suggested it – it was some family name on my grandad's side and she always thought it was pretty.

I walk across the whitewashed wooden floor and take a peek through the slats of a white wooden venetian blind at the window. There's not much of a view out there – looking down, a big old brick building takes up most of a yard that's empty except for a few weeds; looking up, there's a big modern block of flats shutting out most of the summery night sky. I guess the mystery room next door must have the same view.

"So what's in here, Scarlet?" I hear Mum ask, coming to join me.

"Um . . . *your* room?" I suggest.

'Cause this doesn't just look like Mum Heaven by accident, does it? I don't know who or what the inspiration is for the room we just saw, but Nana definitely had Mum in mind when she decorated in here.

And now Mum walks in, looking this way and that in stunned surprise, at the bare, clean loveliness of it.

I leave my mother to absorb the fact that she appears to have her own personalized guest room, and hurry out on to the landing. Mr Spinks seems to know that there's one more place I need to see; he's already plonked on a step of the last staircase – a plainer, narrower set that is lined just on one side with a mismatching collection of old-fashioned china teapots.

Taking the stairs two at a time, I find myself on a miniscule landing in the eaves, the ceiling sloping down on both sides as I face a plain wooden door with a white ceramic doorknob.

I take a breath, turn the handle and quickly feel around the wall to my left. I'm hoping to find a regular light switch, of course, but instead my fingers land on some kind of dangling cable with a switch attached. Hoping I don't get electrocuted, I press it – and at the sound of a soft click, garlands of white fairy lights suddenly pulse all over the almost triangular shape of the wall I'm facing, a wall that's mostly a chimney breast for the fireplaces below. It's painted scarlet red, same as the sloping walls of the roof on either side.

On the sloping wall to the left, a flowery, vintage tea towel is pinned by its four corners, to act as a curtain to a tiny window, I guess. I don't bother to look – it'll have the same across-the-road view of rooftops as Nana's bedroom down below.

Nearly the whole of the polished wooden floor is covered with an old but lovely Persian rug, in shades of rich red and cream.

Mr Spinks trots over it, easily hopping on to the low futon bed with its beautiful, ornately embroidered Indian throw, and turns a few circles before he settles down, panting up at me, as if he's welcoming me to my very own room. Which it is, isn't it? Same as the white one downstairs is Mum's.

"Thank you, Nana," I whisper, staring around at the small but incredibly special attic room.

How lovely, if a little bit sad... Nana and Mum had that final falling-out that broke their relationship, reducing it to a terse "How are you? Fine, thanks," conversation every couple of weeks. And all the time, in her mad new messy venture, Nana had busied herself crafting and creating rooms just for us. For the family that never came.

How stubborn has Mum been, to stay cross with Nana for not listening to her advice?

How stubborn has Nana been, to want us here and never ask?

And how did I never notice before *quite* how useless adults can be?

Thoughts ramble around my already overloaded head, but then my eyes settle on something and my brain suddenly sharpens up.

There, directly above "my" bed, framed by the garlands of fairy lights, is a painting. Small this time. A miniature of the pearl painting in the living room.

Is *this* what Nana wanted me to find?

This *painting* is the pearl in the attic?

I walk closer to it, and lean in to get a better look.

It's incredibly pretty, but it's just … well, *there*. That can't be all, surely?

Then something occurs to me: like all Nana's paintings, it's not a flat picture stuck in a frame; it's canvas stretched over wood, with edges a few centimetres deep.

I reach over and carefully take the pearl painting off the wall.

As soon as I do, a packet of folded cream-coloured papers wrapped with a red ribbon – a scarlet ribbon – drops down from its hiding place at the back of the picture and lands on "my" pillow, making Mr Spinks jump.

With legs a little shaky, I flop down beside Nana's dog.

The pages – covered in that oh-so-recognizable handwriting – rustle and fan out as I free them of the ribbon and folds.

At the same time, a flutter of wings announces the arrival of Angie, who perches on top of the attic door and stares at me.

"Well, well, well!" she caws, in Nana's voice.

Well, well, well, I think too, as I begin to read what's on the paper…

The Pearl in the Attic

By Patsy Jones

Chapter 1

Hornsey, North London, 1904

Ruby tasted blood.

The whole of this long day, she had bitten her lip or nibbled at the skin around her nails till they were raw and ragged. She had drummed her feet, tapped her fingers and twitched at every new sight and sound.

And now she stood by Father's side, feeling unravelled and strange, shivering as if she had been caught standing in the open air dressed in only her vest and drawers.

"Stop," she whispered to herself, fixedly staring down at the pavement, clutching her heavy bag, wishing she could be still, be calm.

But how was that possible?

For today had been the most glorious, wonderful and terrifying of Ruby's entire life.

The long journey on the steam train up from Kent.

Taking the bone-shaking omnibus across the teeming, noisy streets of London.

The final, shorter train ride up to North London, arriving at a station right next to a vast, grand building called Alexandra Palace – owned by which royal person Ruby did not know – set on a hill with views of faraway smoke drifting into the skies from the thousands upon thousands of chimneys of the city beyond.

Now, at the end of this unsettling adventure, they had arrived. And Ruby was about to be handed over like a parcel of meat.

"No, no, NO!" said Father, studying the letter in his hand for the umpteenth time. "This can't be right!"

Ruby kept her gaze downwards, trying to steady her shivering, and said nothing.

It was always better to say nothing.

If you dared to say, "But, Father, I think. . ." you'd have a slap around the head for your cheek, before you even got a chance to say your piece.

They all knew it, all the children.

Ruby swallowed hard, blinking tears away as she pictured her little brothers and sisters back at the farm cottage. They'd been without Mother for half a year now, without Stanley since he was apprenticed to the butcher in Ramsgate. And now that she was here, there'd be no one to come between them and Father. No escape till they were fourteen too, and Father found a position for them far away.

And far away was what mattered to Father. For why, he would say, would a man be so foolish as to have his child find work close by, so that they may still live at home and remain another mouth to feed? No, no ... a live-in position was the key. At least Stanley was only twenty miles from the little ones, and could visit if he chose to. But Ruby was to be placed much further away. Even if she wanted to, she would never be able to find her way back...

"Humrumph! Well, this *should* be Hornsey High Street," Father continued, blocking up the pavement in his stubborn refusal to believe that they were finally at their destination. Ruby tried to shrink into herself, or step this way or that, so as not to inconvenience the bustle of passers-by. Her head held low, she watched black-shod feet trot purposefully by, laden wicker shopping baskets by sides, the wheels of shiny perambulators with squalling babies strapped inside.

And of *course* it was Hornsey High Street, Ruby knew.

When they'd left the train and walked down the great green parks and gardens of Alexandra Palace, they'd followed precisely the directions in Uncle Arthur's letter. Even so, Father had asked a young lad they passed if their route was correct and been told it was. They'd stopped moments ago and gazed up at the sign that read *Hornsey High Street* on the side of a fine tenement building, with a shop beneath it, one of many such buildings, all with shops below, goods piled up or garlanded around their windows.

Father and Ruby were where they were supposed to be, no doubt about it, though Father remained to be convinced.

"And this *is* a baker's shop, but the name is wrong... Why does it say 'Brandt'?" Father grumbled. "It should be 'Wells'."

"You looking for Mr Wells, sir?" asked a voice, and Ruby watched as a bicycle came to a stop beside them, a pair of booted feet expertly bouncing on to the pavement beside it.

She glanced up, drawn by a lad's voice; he sounded as if he might be about the same age as Stanley. He was, give or take a year, she decided when she looked at the scrawny boy, in a second-hand but smart enough black jacket and trousers. The cap on his head was pushed back, and there was sweat on his brow from the exertion of his journeying.

On the front of his delivery bike was a large basket, and down the side, in the most beautiful gilt script, was the name *Brandt – Baker and Confectioner*.

The twinkle of the gilt drew Ruby's eye like a magnet. Richness of colours always stirred something inside her ... the pink-orange sunsets over the Kent cornfields were cheering, their burning glow banishing the day's drudgery. The red sheen and black dots of a ladybird – presented on the fingertip of one of her little siblings – always made Ruby smile. And the lilac haze of lavender fields near the farm; who could ever tire of such a sight?

Ruby had thought of those colours on the train here, knowing they'd be lost to her now, and that nothing could replace them in London's grey cloak of smoke.

But this; this little glimmer of gold ... it gave

Ruby the strength to raise her gaze higher and see what this place was about, this place she must settle in, whether she wanted to or not.

And the look of it quite took her breath away.

As soon as she was old enough to run errands, Ruby had been sent to fetch the family bread from the miller's place, buying a loaf warm and soft from the back door of the bakery shed.

But here was a shop that looked so very grand that Ruby almost expected it to sell fine jewels. Her eyes took in the glossy black of the frontage, with large thick letters above it that read *Brandt – Baker and Confectioner* once again, and once again in that rich gold.

The words were carefully scripted on the huge plate-glass window too, this time in neat golden arches. A door, with a brass bell visible, stood to the right.

As for what lay *inside* the window...

"Oh, my," Ruby murmured, and found herself drawn closer, walking away from her father and the delivery boy. For the window was such a vision! A soft, lustrous purple cloth – velvet, she guessed it to be – was draped all about it, pinned and flowing from some upstanding backing board and pooling into swirls on a wide shelf. Breads and cakes of every shape and size were laid upon it, either spilling out of baskets or displayed on some dainty invention of prettily painted, stacked plates. Ruby had never seen such an abundance, such sweetness . . . and seeing the luxury of it all lit the tiniest flame of hope in Ruby's heart.

Perhaps this position would not be so very awful.

Perhaps her uncle Arthur and his new wife might be kind to her.

She had never met either of them, but they could not be colder or meaner than Father, surely. . . ?

Ruby felt the eyes on her before she saw them.

A woman was staring at Ruby. She stood behind the display in the window, tall, buxom and severe, hair hidden in her white cap, arms crossed in front of her white apron. Was this her aunt . . . her aunt Gertrude?

The woman's look was strange, hard to read. It was not that tight mask of anger that Father wore so very often, nor was it the weary disdain of the old schoolmaster when Ruby smudged her work again.

Before Ruby could fathom what the look could be about, Father's shout drew her attention, and she saw the woman turn away from the window and retreat back into the shop.

"Ruby! This way!" Father ordered her, as a farmer might command his dog.

As Ruby stirred herself, she suddenly understood.

The meaning of the cool, steady look was very clear: *You are not welcome*. . .

Turning slowly, feeling leaden with dread, Ruby went to follow Father and the delivery boy, who was now steering his bicycle through an open doorway that led to a passage next to the shop.

But Ruby found her way blocked by a smiling young woman, her dark hair piled up in fanciful curls. She was dressed most peculiarly, in a waisted navy frock coat and matching long knickerbockers!

"Coming to Alexandra Palace this weekend?" she said, smiling warmly at Ruby and offering her a printed handbill. "I promise, you'll see such things as you've never seen in your whole life. A Wild West show, I tell you, with the one and only, world-famous Colonel Samuel Cody!"

This Colonel Samuel Cody might very well be world famous, but not in Ruby's small patch of England. She squinted at the handbill held out to her, making out nothing of the smaller printed words beyond blackened smudges against the paper, though the title *SF Cody and Company* and the drawing under it was just about clear enough. The coloured drawing was of a man in a hat like that of some cowboy, with long hair, a raggedy beard, twirled moustache and fringed jacket. He sat upon a horse that was rearing up, its front legs tearing at the air. In one hand the man held the horse's reins, while in the other he held . . . a gun!

The grip of Father's fingers suddenly dug painfully into Ruby's arm, and she was tugged roughly away.

"Come see me fly off into the sky!" the girl called after her cheerfully.

Tripping and stumbling, Ruby wondered what the girl could possibly mean by that, but had not the luxury of time to dwell on the matter.

The gate to the alleyway banged shut behind Ruby with the heavy certainty of a prison door, locking the girl and her bright words in the sunshine outside.

In the gloom of the passageway, Ruby bit her lip, and felt buried. . .

Two (Surprises) for the Price of One

"Who knew she'd be as good at writing as she is at painting?" I ask in wonder, my mind still reeling with the delicious find of Nana's story last night. Or at least, the first chapter of it.

Mr Spinks gazes up at me but doesn't reply. Maybe it's because it was a rhetorical question, or maybe it's because he's busy weeing up against a street lamp.

"Do you think she's written more?" I ask, just enjoying the novelty of having a dog to hang out with. "I've *got* to find out what happened to poor Ruby. . ."

I'd reread the pages a heap of times before I went to sleep last night, half expecting to lose myself in tangled dreams about Ruby and the future she faced.

But I think so much had gone on in such a short time with Nana and, well, *everything*, that my subconscious was spoiled for choice when it came to stuff to mull over while I slept.

In fact, it was a pretty busy night in Dreamland...

Dream One. I was fighting my way through a dark forest of trees made of boxes, till I heard the *THWACK! THWACK!* of axes and saw cardboard trunks begin to crash down on top of me.

Dream Two. I was running up Nana's book-strewn staircase, but like a downward-bound escalator, I was going nowhere fast, with pages fluttering and flying all around my head.

Dream Three. I'd been dyeing Nana's hair mermaid blue, but first her hair and then *Nana* had disappeared, slipping clean away through my fingers...

But this morning the sun is shining, and I feel a bit better and a bit brighter.

Hornsey High Street looks a bit better and brighter too, in daylight. On my way to this grassy little green that Mr Spinks has just dragged me to, I spotted a florist bursting with colour and a café with pretty hanging baskets all around it.

"Hey, I forgot; Nana said to tell you she's fine,"
I say, staring down at Mr Spinks. "And that what
happened wasn't your fault."

Mr Spinks wags his tail like fury. Does he
understand, or does he think I have some doggy
treats in my pocket? It's like two people who speak
different languages trying to get by via the universal
language of hopeful smiles.

"Suppose we'd better get back," I tell him, then
see that a passing mum and kid are grinning at
me.

Uh-oh ... talking out loud to a dog is obviously a
sign of mild madness. But how would I know? Like
I say, I'm totally new at this pet-care lark.

But pet care is one of the reasons me and Mum
didn't go back to our own place last night. Plus
the fact that Mum couldn't face the long drive to
Chelmsford, not after the shock of Nana's. . .

a)   fall
b)   diagnosis
c)   hoarding mania
d)   unexpected pets that we were suddenly
     responsible for.

And so we'd stayed in the rooms Nana had prepared for us – and when I say prepared, I mean right down to pyjamas under the pillows ... white cotton ones for Mum, a grey nightshirt with "TEAM UNICORN" on it for me.

(Were the ready-and-waiting rooms just Nana being optimistic, and hoping the cold war between her and Mum would ease off soon? Or a symptom of Nana being fuzzy around the edges...?)

I slept pretty well, though when I got up in the night to use the loo (a freaky experience with a basket of plastic ducks staring at me, like birdy convicts) I saw that Mum was still awake. She was firing off emails on her ever-present iPad to everyone at work, telling them that she couldn't come in today and giving them a thousand orders, I bet, about what they should and shouldn't do in her absence.

She'd already dropped an email to the school's attendance officer, letting her know that I wouldn't be in. All I'd be missing was last-day-of-term stuff like movies and quizzes in lessons. And having an excuse to avoid Miss Kendrick after sending in that useless bit of Spanish homework sounded pretty good to me...

Anyway, I've learned my lesson about talking out loud to dogs, so me and Mr Spinks mooch along the pavement in comfy silence till we're directly opposite Nana's flat, and the derelict shop below it.

"Sit!" I say, since a direct doggy order shouldn't look too bonkers.

Mr Spinks *doesn't* sit, but he does look up at me in a smiley sort of way and wags his tail a bit faster.

While we wait for a gap in the traffic, I gaze over at the shop, imagining the fictional Ruby standing there, wondering what was to become of her, what her life would be like working at Brandt's Bakery and Confectioners.

Actually, was it *really* a baker's shop back in 1904? Did Nana know that for sure? Or had she just invented it for the sake of her story?

Alexandra Palace is definitely real – when I showed Mum Chapter One of *The Pearl in the Attic* last night, she said it was round here somewhere, the building, the park, though she wasn't sure if the station actually existed, or if Nana had made that part up.

I have to say, I was kind of disappointed that Mum wasn't more interested in the story, but I think she thought of it just as another of Nana's projects, alongside painting and collecting vast amounts of vintage and non-vintage tat and junk. She'd only smiled absent-mindedly and said, "Ruby red, Scarlet red . . . maybe Nana named the character in honour of *you*, using the closest historical equivalent to your name."

But I suppose Mum had been a bit distracted when we got back from the hospital, what with sorting out work stuff and googling "dementia". . .

A toot of a car horn and some flashing lights gets my attention, and I see someone's been kind enough to stop and let me and Mr Spinks cross while the traffic's at a standstill. We run, and run again once we get inside, Mr Spinks leaping up the stairs incredibly speedily for one so short and pudgy.

"We're back!" I call out, as we go through the top door and into the flat.

"Hi!" Mum calls out from the kitchen.

"Hello!" Angie squawks from the top of a box tower.

"Careful – don't trip over the bag in the doorway," says Mum as I slink sideways past boxes in an attempt to get to the kitchen.

"What's in it?" I ask, staring down at a holdall that's probably stuffed with something ridiculous, like antique rolling pins or a collection of *Guinness World Records* annuals from the 1980s.

"It's just a few things for Nana," says Mum. "She called from the hospital while you were out and asked me to bring her toiletries, her phone, pyjamas and some art stuff."

Now that I've negotiated the obstacle course of the hall and am finally in the kitchen, I see that Mum is standing in front of an open cupboard. Lots of open cupboards, actually.

"What are you doing?" I ask her.

"I was looking for breakfast cereal, but I found this instead," she says, her hands on her hips, weariness written on her face.

The shelves are neatly stacked, I'll give Nana that. But instead of tins of beans and packets of pasta, there are balls and balls and *balls* of coloured wool in one cupboard; old jam jars full of coloured buttons, beads and crafting bits and bobs in another; and the one above the fridge is packed with nothing but glue. Glue tubs, glue tubes, glue sticks, glitter glue. . .

"Not so great for breakfast," I say. "It's really hard to get glitter out from between your teeth, even *with* flossing."

Mum rolls her eyes at me, and slams shut the cupboard doors one by one, which gets Mr Spinks yelping excitedly and sends Angie squawking and flying off to the sanctuary of her cage.

Tink! Tinkle! Tink!

Mum drops her head and shuts her eyes. She's counting to ten, and probably hoping at the end of it she'll open them and find herself in her neat, calm office, and that the last twelve hours will all have been a dream. . .

"Shall we grab a croissant at the hospital?" I suggest, trying to be helpful, since I can't exactly make Nana's mess disappear or the whole nightmare go away.

"Yep," says Mum, snapping into Practical Mode and grabbing the car keys.

Twenty minutes later, we get to the hospital. Half an hour after *that*, we finally find a parking space.

(I lost count of the number of times Mum growled, "You have GOT to be joking!" when we turned into yet *another* jam-packed road.)

"Oh, I'm a such a mess!" Mum mutters, smoothing her hair in the reflection of the glass in the revolving door of the hospital entrance.

"No, you're not," I tell her, though to be honest, my normally hyper-perfect mum *is* looking a little crumpled around the edges.

I catch sight of myself in the glass and spot that I'm a little crumpled around the edges too. But that's not much of a shock, since I'm mostly *always* pretty scruffy. Same as Mum, I'm still in yesterday's clothes, only I've swapped my black hoodie for this pink tweed vintage jacket I found on one of the clothes racks on the top landing. It looks great with my hair. (Bella and Aisha would be horrified to the point of barfing at the idea of me wearing "smelly" second-hand stuff.)

"Argh! Look at the time; if it hadn't taken us so long to find a stupid parking space. . ." Mum moans, as the revolving door steers us into the airy reception area, with its information desk, lifts and escalators and sweet, sharp scent of disinfectant.

It's not technically visiting time, but Mum phoned ahead and got special permission, since she had to have the meeting with the other doctor and someone from social services. Plus, as Mum pointed out, an early visit meant we could leave straight after and zip back to Chelmsford for fresh clothes, plus rubber gloves to clean Nana's flat when we got back. Mum says we'll have to stay in London for the weekend at least, till we see what's what.

"Listen, Scarlet, I'm going to have to go straight to the meeting," Mum says wearily as she checks her watch. "Are you all right to go and sit with Nana on your own till I come? And can you give her this?"

"Sure," I say, taking the holdall Mum packed earlier.

I'd really like to have time on my own with Nana, to be honest. Now that I've had a glimpse of the upside-down world she was living in without us knowing, I feel really protective of her. I also realize how much I've missed her. Growing up, hanging out with Nana felt like hanging out with the most fun, adult-sized kid, who'd make up the best games and giggle as much as me – while Mum would be in the background rolling her eyes at both of us.

"Good girl. Love you," says Mum, giving me a quick kiss on the cheek before she rushes off to a close-by lift that's just opened its doors.

Well. *That* was a bit surprising. The "good girl" bit and the "love you" and the kiss, I mean. Mum doesn't usually say or do any of those things. And I don't do them back.

But I quite like that it just happened, I realize, as I bound up the short escalator that'll take me to the section of the building with the wards in it. It's funny, but I think Mum and me have talked more in the last few hours than we have in the last few weeks put together. It's like we've had to become a team overnight or something. Which *sounds* a bit corny, but *feels* sort of good, to be honest. . .

Anyway, Nana is the most important person in all this, and now that I'm getting closer to Ward 9, I start to hurry, keen to get to her and tell her all the things I lay in bed thinking about, after the dawn light came glowing through the tea-towel curtain in the small window in the sloped ceiling.

For a start, I want to let her know that I LOVE my attic room.

And I think she'll *love* to know that Mr Spinks is fine and kept me company – and sniggering – all night on the bottom of my bed as he zzzzzz-ed and snurfled in his sleep.

I want to tell her that I think Angie likes me; she let me put her in her cage last night (with the lure of a grape) and sang me "Twinkle, Twinkle Little Star" when I let her out this morning.

I want to ask Nana who Dean and baby Zephyr

are, since me and Mum didn't come across any pet/ gremlin/alien in the flat by that name.

But most of all, I want to tell her I *adored* the story she wrote. I've brought Chapter One of *The Pearl in the Attic* with me in my backpack so we can chat about it. And of course, I need to know if there's more; I HAVE to find out what happened to poor, uprooted, unwelcome Ruby!

Fancy my gran having a go at writing a novel, I think as I buzz into the ward and walk towards her bed. Maybe she'll get it published and go on book tours. Except that's not very likely, I quickly remind myself, if the diagnosis turns out to be right. . .

I take a deep breath and wipe away the tears, so Nana will see the cheeriest version of me that I can—

Oh.

I slow down.

Considering it's not visiting time, I'm a bit surprised to see two figures sitting on the orange plastic chairs either side of Nana's bed. The one with his face to me is quite young: a tanned, sandy-haired teenage boy, with a brown-beaded necklace showing above the neck of his faded T-shirt. The darker-haired figure with his back to me shields my view of the person in the bed, who can't be Nana.

But a couple of tentative steps on, I see that it is.

Nana is looking confused, probably wondering who these strange people are.

I'd better help.

"Nana?" I say, reaching the bottom of her bed.

"Well, well, well!" she says, breaking into a smile. "My sweet Scarlet! Where's your mum?"

"Um. . ." I fumble, not totally sure what I should or shouldn't say. "She's having a meeting with another doctor, but don't worry, she'll be here soon."

"Another doctor? What about? Should I be in the meeting too?" says the person opposite the teenage boy. He's a grown man – dark eyes, dark hair, Anglo-Indian, maybe? But with an accent that sounds Australian, I'm pretty sure. He's dressed in a worn checked shirt and jeans and looks like he just finished lumberjacking or something.

"It's just for family," I say quickly.

"But sweetheart, Dean IS family!" says Nana, looking at me with her piercingly blue eyes.

Dean? *DEAN*?!?

"Who? How!" I bumblingly ask, completely thrown at hearing one of the names Nana came out with yesterday.

"Hi, how are you, Scarlet," says the man, holding out his hand to shake mine. Dumbly, I shake it back, though I haven't a clue what's happening. "Patsy has told us lots about you. All good! But I get the feeling she hasn't told you much about us. . . ?"

I look from the smiling man to the slightly embarrassed-looking boy to Nana.

"Nana mentioned you yesterday," I find myself babbling. "She said she was worried the hospital would wake you up . . . you and baby Zephyr."

What I've said – it makes the man and the boy burst out laughing. Even Nana is laughing, but putting her hands up to her face in embarrassment.

I can't remember a time I felt less in on a joke.

"Oh, I was *very* muddled yesterday, wasn't I?" says Nana. "I even called myself by my old married name when they checked me in here! Couldn't think *why* the nurse was calling me Mrs Chaudhary this morning. I said to her, 'What silly sausage went and told you *that* was my name?' and of course she said, 'YOU, dear!' Ha!"

Everyone's laughing again – except me.

"Yeah, but Nana, I still don't get it."

"Which part, darling?" Nana asks, making me feel like I'm having a mind-twisting conversation with the Mad Hatter. "You mean why I thought they'd disturb Dean if they called last night?"

I answer her with a suppose-so shrug. I'd rather find out who Dean actually *is*, but this piece of information might help us get there.

"Well, because I was all in a muddle with the shock and the painkillers, I thought Dean was over in Australia, and in a different time zone, but of course he was already in here in Britain. And Zephyr ... well, in my mind I was thinking of the picture on the mantelpiece, when Zeph was a baby and in his grandad Manny's arms. But you're hardly a baby, are you, Zeph!"

Nana smiles warmly at the tanned teen boy.

I don't understand a word of this explanation.

I also don't know why the tanned teen boy who is Zephyr suddenly looks familiar.

"We live in Melbourne, Australia, but I had to go to a work convention here in the UK, in Cornwall. I took Zeph out of school to come with me – he's always wanted to see the beaches there!" this Dean person says. "We'd planned to come to London and visit Patsy in a couple of days' time, but when the hospital phoned and told me what had happened, we just packed up our stuff and jumped in the hire car."

Dean's sing-song Australian accent is bright and breezy, but I still fix him with my version of Mum's fierce glower. I might not know what this stranger's on about, but it does sound an awful lot like he's staking some sort of claim on my gran.

"Nana," I say, turning sharply to her. "*Please* explain what's going on!"

"Oh, Scarlet, darling, don't look so grumpy!" she pleads. "It's all pretty straightforward. Dean is . . . I suppose he's my. . ."

Nana wafts her good hand in the air as she struggles for the right term. It doesn't come.

"I don't think what *we* are *has* a name," Dean says warmly to her.

"Yeah, but me and Scarlet are cousins, right?" the boy suddenly chips in.

"No, we're not!" I immediately snap, feeling my pale cheeks heat up with outrage.

"Um, technically, you are," says Dean, shrugging his shoulders almost apologetically. "Your mum is my half-sister. Ren and I have the same dad – Mandeep Chaudhary?"

"Ah, Manny, Manny, Manny. . ." Nana says wistfully, as if she's playing a scratchy old Super 8 film in her head of the young, happy couple she and my grandad once were.

As I stare at Nana, and at this person who is, I guess, my ... my *uncle,* I find myself wondering, did I ever know my grandad's first name? I don't think I did. It never seemed relevant; I've never met him. Mum hasn't seen him since she was a little kid, since she and Nana left Australia and came back to Britain.

Neither Nana or Mum ever talked about him much. "It's sad, but me and your grandad just grew apart, Scarlet, and it was kinder to let each other go," Nana told me cheerfully once when I was young. "As I've always told your mother, never regret the past, but always look forward!"

But here he is, this unknown grandad, creeping *out* of the past and affecting my world.

After all, he's the reason my tiny family appears to have increased by two-fifths overnight... Or fifty per cent, if you count Grandad Manny too, I suppose.

I think my "uncle" Dean has noticed my knuckles turning white as I clutch the metal rail at the bottom of the bed. He gets up and ushers me to sit down in his place. I don't know what to do or what to think of this new information, but I know I feel a bit weak and so I shuffle over, let my little backpack and Nana's holdall thunk to the floor and sink into the plastic seat with a "thank you" that's about as squeaky as a kitten's mew.

"Look, I think I'd better go and find out about this meeting . . . and introduce myself to your mum!" Dean says to me, before beaming broadly at Nana and his son. "Zeph – I won't be long. And Patsy, don't go dancing around the room while I'm gone. You need your rest!"

Nana bursts into girlish giggles and waves off Dean's silliness as he hurries out of the ward. I notice one of her gemstone hair clips is hanging loose in her upswept waves. I'd reach over and fix it before it falls, but I'm feeling too cross with her to care.

As she turns back to me, she spots that I'm not exactly going along with the jollity.

"Look, it's a lot to take in, I know, Scarlet, darling," she says, her smile slipping, a look of concern replacing it.

"Well, yeah!" I blurt out. "I mean, when did all *this* happen?"

I agitatedly sweep my hands out over the bed,

over the bump of plaster and metal pins that are holding Nana together.

I spot the boy on the other side of the bed shuffle in his seat, his two hands tucked between his knees, awkwardness obvious in his body language.

"The thing is, Scarlet, your grandad Manny remarried a few years after me and your mum came back to Britain, and he went on to have a new family," Nana starts to explain, but *this* part I get. Of course Grandad Manny or whatever his name is had gone on to have a new family, or I wouldn't have just met and been introduced to an unexpected Australian uncle and cousin.

"My grandad – *our* grandad – passed away last year," says the boy on the other side of the bed.

Oh… I make a mental note to bring my new family total back to two-fifths of an increase.

"But before he died," my "cousin" carries on, "he made Dad promise he'd find Patsy and Ren. Grandad always thought about them, always felt really sad about losing touch."

Patsy and Ren.

Not Patsy and Ren and *Scarlet*, of course, since my grandfather didn't know I existed. Which is quite a weird feeling, suddenly.

"Listen, darlings," says Nana, gazing from Zephyr to me and back again. "It's wonderful to see you, but I'm absolutely worn out. Can you maybe leave me to have a sleep, and come back for a visit later in the day?"

Now I feel a little sad and swizzed... I'd planned on having a lovely conversation with Nana, just the two of us, and it has been completely hijacked, in the hugest of ways.

Her eyes are already closing, and I haven't been able to ask her if she thinks I suit the pink jacket I borrowed.

I haven't been able to thank her for the excellent TEAM UNICORN nightie.

I haven't been able to ask her how she ended up with Mr Spinks and Angie.

I haven't been able to tell her about keeping my promise and finding her story...

"So, shall we get out of here?" I hear my so-called cousin ask.

I look up and see that Zephyr's standing, and is gripping a wheelie suitcase in each hand. He lets go of one momentarily, to push his tousled, sandy hair off his tanned face.

And *then* I know why this boy with the bizarre name seemed familiar.

I've seen him before – on a wave, on a surfboard, on the wall of the middle bedroom of Nana's flat.

The painting; the twin beds in that room; the suitcases Zephyr's holding.

Uh-oh. Are me and Mum about to have flatmates...?

You have GOT to be joking, I think, since Mum's not around to say it.

"Bye, Nana," I say out loud instead, as I turn away, Zephyr rumbling ominously behind me with his luggage.

And then I hear Nana's voice.

"Scarlet, come here a second!" she calls out, and beckons me back to her bedside.

Leaving Zephyr by the ward door, I scurry back to her, and see her blue eyes are twinkling as if she has the most excellent secret.

"I didn't want to ask in front of anyone, but did you find it?"

"Yes!" I blurt out, knowing exactly what she means. "I found the first part of your story behind the painting in the—"

Nana puts her finger to her lips, as if there might be spies everywhere, even though the lady in the bed next to her seems engrossed in a copy of *Hello* magazine and doesn't seem much of a security risk.

"I asked your mother to pack my sketchbook," says Nana, giving a nod to the holdall on the floor. "Is it in there? Can you pass it to me, sweetheart?"

"Uh, sure," I say, wondering if changing subjects practically mid-sentence is a symptom of dementia.

In amongst the fluffy pyjamas, washbag, mobile phone and charger, I find the hardback A4 book she must be talking about. It's neon orange with a matching elastic fabric band holding it shut.

"Are you going to do some drawing while you're in here?" I ask, wondering if Mum's packed pencils for Nana too.

"No, it's for *you*," says Nana. "Now shoo – go and look after Zephyr. The poor boy's looking lost!"

He's not the only one, I think, staring down at the chunky book in my hand.

"Night, night," she jokes as her sleepy eyes begin to close.

Then one opens, just as I'm about to leave.

"Writing's an art form, isn't it?" she says with a small, sly smile.

And then I get it.

The fact that Nana has just given me Chapter Two, I'm pretty sure! Now as I look at the sketchbook side-on I can see that there's something folded between the pages, and a little flash of red ribbon...

"Thank you," I say, though she seems to be asleep already, or doing a pretty good impression anyway.

"Is Patsy all right?" asks Zephyr as I catch him up.

"Yep," I say, clutching the sketchbook to my chest. I have no idea what Nana's doing, doling out these sections of her book in such a mysterious way – but I have to admit, it's kind of fun.

"So, what should we do? Go to the café or something?" Zephyr suggests uncertainly.

"Sure. Meet you there," I say, and then instantly disappear into the nearest ladies' loos.

Zephyr can think I'm rude if he likes, but I'm planning on spending the next five minutes in a twenty-first-century toilet cubicle, being transported to a cake shop in 1904...

The Pearl in the Attic

Chapter 2

Welcome.

It was a word that came easily to Mother.

Welcome, to the charitable ladies who sometimes stopped by with gifts of old clothes or food.

You're welcome, to the pedlars who might pass by, selling none of their few wares to a woman with no money, but getting a mug of tea for the brief pleasure of their conversation.

Welcome, one and all, stitched into a tapestry Mother made when she was a young, bright thing, and now hanging over the dark, smoking fireplace at the cottage where she sat no more.

Welcome.

It was not a word Ruby expected to hear again, for a very long time, if at all...

"I said *shift* yourself!" A roar broke into her rememberings as she followed Father and the boy with the bike, her bag bashing against her leg, the alleyway leading them through to a small, shaded yard, with a new brick building taking up most of it. Heat and steam and white dust surged out of a thrown-wide door.

"Mr Wells?" the boy shouted as he propped the bike against a wall. "Visitors for you!"

There was no reply; the clattering of machinery within drowned out the boy's voice.

"Arthur?" Father called out, stepping inside.

Ruby was too wary to follow. Instead she hovered near the doorway, aware of the delivery boy's watchful eyes, filled with burrowing curiosity, looking her up and down.

Avoiding his gaze, she stared inside the bakery – and was startled. For a place of such rough work it was a very fine, very large room.

The walls were of white tile, placed one atop another, mimicking brickwork. There were long tables – some of wood, some of marble – positioned here and there, with brass scales set upon them, and copper pans in the most curious shapes. Jars too, but what was in them Ruby could not guess at.

And most impressive was a great, square, iron box, almost the size of a small room itself, which sat at the back of the building. Foot-high doors were peppered over its surface, and Ruby quickly saw what they were for: a tall, sullen-looking man in a white apron and a puffed white hat threw one of the doors open and pulled out a long paddle of wood, with good-smelling rolls along the length of it. It was some modern type of bread oven, Ruby realized, thinking of the lumpen, brick, coal-fired contraptions in the miller's shed back home.

"Eric!" came a roar, and Ruby leant forward a little, to see a big man – also in a white apron and puffed hat – grapple her father in a manner more akin to the wrestling of boys in a schoolyard fight. "So you're finally here, eh? What do you make of my place? A fine establishment, is it not?"

As her father and his brother broke apart, Ruby saw the ruddiness of Uncle Arthur's cheeks. Of course, the flush of them could be caused by the heat of the bakery, but a darkening bloom about his cheeks and nose set Ruby thinking of the men who would sit hour after hour in the tavern in the village, spending their earnings on ale and port that was meant for their children's supper. Men who'd shout or hit out at those very children, sent by their mothers to try and fetch home their fathers, dear fathers.

"It is indeed!" Ruby's own father nodded in agreement, gazing about him. "But why is not 'Wells' on the signage? Why does it say that German-sounding nonsense?"

"Ah, Brandt is the name of my wife's first husband," Uncle Arthur explained with a sneer. "He spent a pretty penny on the decoration of the shop before he died, but *I'm* the one to take advantage of it. I have his business, his wife and his profits. And I'm not fool enough to waste my money painting it over!"

"But we're being overrun by immigrants in this country," Father grumbled. "Especially the *Germans*. You don't want folk to think you're one of them, do—"

A cough stopped Father in his tracks.

It came from just behind Ruby, and she turned to see the woman she'd spotted inside the shop.

The woman paid no heed to Ruby, but came to stand beside her.

Her expressionless gaze was aimed at Ruby's father. The very blankness of it once again seemed to say *You're not welcome*. Ruby was relieved to see this unspoken message was not only directed at her.

"Eric," said Uncle Arthur, "this is Gertrude."

Gertrude. . . Ruby rolled the name around silently on her tongue. Of course, it was a German name too. No wonder her aunt's nostrils flared just a very little when Ruby's father strode over to shake her hand.

"A pleasure to meet you," Father lied, his face a picture of dislike at having to greet his brother's new, foreign-born wife.

Aunt Gertrude said nothing in response, but limply shook the offered hand and made the tiniest of head bobs. Ruby wondered for a moment if she even spoke English.

"So Gertie runs the shop, of course, with the help of Nell when it's busy, though we'll have to get rid of *her*," Uncle Arthur announced matter-of-factly. "And *I* have Wilfred in here with me making the bread while I do the cakes. He's simple-minded but he'll do. Then there's the lad Billy on deliveries, and a charwoman that comes in to do the heavy cleaning. So I'm quite the success, eh, Eric?"

Uncle Arthur punched Father on the arm several times during his boasting, as if to make sure Father knew his place, simple farm worker that he was.

"Indeed you are," Father admitted, his jaw a little clenched.

"So, now then, Eric, we should get Billy to fetch us some ale to have together before you return home," bellowed Uncle Arthur, puffing himself up in his obvious gloating and pride. "But first, what have you got for me?"

Ruby stood still as she was able, unaware of picking at the skin around a nail, as she waited to hear what Father was meant to have brought for her uncle. It was only when first Father, and then Uncle Arthur, turned to stare her way that Ruby realized the item was *her*.

"So this is my eldest girl," Father announced, waving a hand vaguely towards Ruby. "She's fairly strong, and doesn't need much feeding. You'll find her manner docile enough."

Ruby raged quietly inside at being discussed as if she were a calf being sold at market. But her thoughts and feelings hunkered under her skin, visible to no one, showing only an outward calm that hid the volcano boiling beneath.

"Well, I'm taking the girl on as a favour to you, Eric, but she'd better do as she's told, or she'll be out of here faster than she can blink," said Uncle Arthur, inspecting Ruby and seeming to find her wanting. "I've neither the money nor the patience to look after other people's children, as if I'm a house of charity or—"

"Come," interrupted Aunt Gertrude, turning to go in a rustle of stiff skirts.

Ruby was torn for a moment, till she saw Billy widen his eyes at her and chuck his head in the direction of the departing Aunt Gertrude, who was walking towards an open back door of the main building and clearly expecting Ruby to follow.

"She's not to have the good guest room, mind!" Uncle Arthur shouted after his wife as Ruby hurried after her. "You'll put her in the attic, as I told you!"

"I will *not*," Ruby heard her aunt mutter under her breath, and watched as the big woman in front lifted her skirts and stamped away from the bakery, the yard and her husband.

Entering the building, a sweet-smelling but gloomy room greeted Ruby; her eyes strained to make sense of the stacked shelves of produce and sacks of flour piled up against the walls.

Then Aunt Gertrude walked through a connecting door into a room that was flooded in the most beautiful golden light.

Ruby, still clutching her bag of belongings, gazed around at the shop. Three connecting counters faced the door and velvet-lined window that she had seen from the pavement outside.

On the walls behind were dark wooden shelves upon shelves, laden with breads and rolls in shapes Ruby had never seen before: long, twisted sticks; large domes with smaller domes on top; curious six-sided loaves that appeared more like a cake of some kind; plaited breads curiously shaped into horseshoes.

Ruby could see them all clear as day, thanks to wall-mounted gas mantles which cast their light stronger than any candle, and made a hissing noise as if there were snakes curled around their brass mouldings and frosted shades.

And what she could see in the glass-fronted counters ... oh, the dainty cakes that were there! Flaky cones of pastry oozed cream and dripped with jam. Thick-cut slabs of sponge the colour of corn yellow, rose pink and grass green. Amber-tinted tarts festooned with real fruit; ruby-hued tarts festooned with fruit made from some kind of sugared, coloured sweets.

In the largest of the displays, huge, triumphant,

many-layered cakes heaved with colour and decoration. Ruby's eyes darted from one to the other, unable to take in the beauty and delicious details before her.

She strived to drink in every vivid shade, every twinkle of detail, every scent of sugared sweetness, before she was banished from this palace and made to skivvy in the drab home of her uncle.

"Have you worked a cash register before?" Aunt Gertrude demanded, positioning herself by some kind of machine resting on top of the counter, like a small, squat metal piano, painted black and gold, with an array of pistons and pads attached to the front of it.

"No," said Ruby, shuffling shyly over to see what this mechanical beast was.

As she did so, for the first time she noticed a young, tired-looking woman stand up from behind a counter, the empty tray in her hand not quite hiding a roundness of her belly.

"A pity," sighed Aunt Gertrude, in a lightly accented but obviously weary voice. "Well, it is simple to learn. Each of the keys here have a price on them, see? You can add up the costings of every item a customer chooses."

Ruby squinted at the numbers on the pads her aunt was pointing to, trying to make them out.

"What is wrong?" Aunt Gertrude suddenly snapped. "Have you had no schooling? Don't you know your numbers?"

Ruby felt a hot flush of shame as her aunt and the pregnant young woman stared at her.

"I – I – I know my numbers well enough, just as long as they are writ large," Ruby stammered.

"Hmmph," muttered Aunt Gertrude. "Well, you'd better learn the costings and the register fast, or you'll be no use to me in the shop. But come on – I'll take you up to your room and you can leave your bags there before we show you how things are done."

The shame of her poor eyesight in close work faded as Ruby obediently went to follow her aunt out of the tinkling front door of the shop.

What does this mean? Ruby wondered as Aunt Gertrude immediately turned into a recessed doorway next to the shop, and searched for a key on the burgeoning metal ring of different-sized keys tied to a belt round her waist.

Was Ruby not destined to be a maid-of-all-work, as she and her father had supposed? Was she to be a *shop* girl instead?

Ruby bit her already tender lip as thoughts and possibilities flew around her mind. She was *not* to empty chamber pots, then? To endlessly blacken the stove and fireplaces on her knees? To stitch and mend with eyes that could not manage such neat work, no matter how much she struggled and toiled?

Ruby was to serve customers. To dress smartly. To be around those cakes that were like pieces of art.

Was this not something? Was this not hope?

And then Ruby saw the marks.

As Aunt Gertrude lifted the key to the door, the cotton sleeve of her blouse rode up her arm, and a purple-blue pattern on her skin revealed itself, matching the fading lilac of the bruise Ruby could now plainly see on the woman's jaw.

A sharp breeze picked up, sending a crumpled handbill tumbling along the pavement, taking Ruby's fragile hopes with it. . .

Not Pleased to Meet You

Crunch, crunch, crunch.

"Sure you don't want one?" Zephyr asks, rustling a packet of crisps he must've just bought from the vending machine.

I tap my fingers on the sketchbook on my lap, wishing I was somewhere quiet, somewhere alone, so I could reread Chapter Two, and soak up every delicious description of the cake shop Ruby found herself in.

Would it be rude – or weird – to disappear off to the ladies' loos again so soon? I only came back and joined Zephyr a minute ago.

Still, I *am* tempted to scuttle off, and it's not just because of the chapter that's tucked inside Nana's sketchbook. The thing is, I'm not really sure what me and Zephyr are meant to say to each other. It's pretty embarrassing hanging out with a strange boy, with a strange name, who I'm supposed to be related to. But I suppose Mum is in exactly the same position, in a doctor's office somewhere in this building.

And I guess it doesn't help that my bum is on the seat of a hard chair in the hospital café, but my head is still drifting in Edwardian London.

"Nope," I reply to his offer of Quavers.

I drum my fingers on the orange sketchbook in my lap and then glance at my mobile, willing Mum to get back to my text. *Nana sleeping – we are in hospital café. Come soon! S* x I'd typed on my way here from the loo just now.

"I could *never* live in a place like this."

"A hospital?" I say, glancing up at Zephyr.

I could pretend I'm being funny, just fooling around like Nana would do, but of course my humour is armed with barbs.

"London, I mean!" says Zephyr, laughing along, not spotting the edge to my voice. "It's *way* too big and busy. It's just packed with roads and traffic."

I think for a second, trying to remember the name

of the place that Nana and Grandad had emigrated to; where Mum was born.

"Isn't Melbourne a big city?" I ask.

"Yeah, but we live outside of it. Near the beach."

"You're into surfing," I say, thinking of the painting in the room back at Nana's flat.

"Yeah, that's why I wanted to come with Dad when he went to Cornwall – I've heard so much about the surfing beaches there," says Zephyr, shoving some more crisps in his mouth. Then he glances up at me. "Hey, how did you know I was into surfing? I thought you didn't know anything about me and my family!"

"I didn't. I mean, I don't really." I fumble for my words. "It's just that there's this picture of you that Nana painted—"

"Oh, yeah!" Zephyr interrupts, his face lighting up. "I can't wait to see that for real. Patsy's an amazing artist, isn't she? I mean, I emailed her that shot a couple of weeks ago, and then when she showed me the painting, finished and up on the wall of—"

"Wait," I say, doing the interrupting this time. "How could she have shown it to you? You've only just arrived here..."

Zephyr blinks his brown eyes at me, as if he can't believe I could be so dumb.

"Well, Skype, of course! Patsy likes giving us a guided tour of the place. Showing us her latest paintings, and what mad stuff she's bought. We like when she does close-ups of Mr Spinks and Angie too."

"You and your dad Skype Nana? Since when?" I demand, feeling a little rumble of jealousy in my chest. I'm jealous that they know Nana, and that they've seen her flat *way* before I saw it. I'm even jealous that they're buddy-buddy with the stupid dog and parrot. Who I'm really, really fond of already, actually.

"Well, since Dad managed to track Patsy down a few months ago ... I guess we talk maybe once a week?"

"You and your dad talk to her that often?" I ask, alternating between a flush of rage and a chill of sadness that someone else has been chatting to my grandmother when it should have been *me*.

"Sure. Us two, and my mum and my little sister, Missy, sometimes," Zephyr says with a shrug.

SLAM! I have more relatives. An aunt and another cousin, it seems. My head is so twisty I can't even do the family maths any more...

"So," Zephyr mumbles with his mouth full, "how did you guys fall out with Patsy anyway?"

BLAM! Zephyr's question is like a slap.

How can he ask a question like that when he doesn't even know us? And why do I need to explain Mum and Nana's eternally tetchy relationship to him anyway? I feel like slapping him back.

"You *do* know my grandmother – *our* grandmother – has dementia, don't you?"

As soon as I say it, as soon as I see his reaction, I feel awful.

"No *way*!" he exclaims, slamming back in his chair. "I just thought she was a bit, you know, *kooky*. In a brilliant way. I can't believe she's—"

"Scarlet!"

I have never been so glad to see my mother.

She's hurrying over to me, a few steps ahead of Zephyr's dad. I feel I'm some oasis she's trying to reach, after being lost in the desert for days.

"All right, darling?" she says, wrapping an arm around me and planting a quick kiss on my head before she sits down in the chair next to me.

"Mmm," I mumble, blushing a little at Mum's unexpected warmth, and not just because it's happened in public.

Then I see her take a deep breath, sit a little taller, and get herself into Practical Mode.

"Well, this is quite a day," she says, raising her dark eyebrows a little. "So, Zephyr; you and Scarlet have already met, but we haven't. I'm Ren. Your *aunt* Ren, I suppose."

She holds out a hand to shake Zephyr's, at a tricky point in his snack eating. My cousin quickly shoves a handful of crisps into his mouth, then offers his salty, greasy fingers to Mum.

"Sorry, I appear to have failed to teach my son any manners," says Dean, grinning as he intervenes, grabbing a serviette from the dispenser on the table and placing it firmly into Zephyr's hands. "Anyway, Scarlet, as you can tell, I've managed to fill your mum in. You know, surprise, surprise – we're related!"

I look from Dean to Mum, who is giving her unexpected half-brother a pursed, small smile. To anyone who doesn't know Mum, she might be exuding calm, but *I'm* thinking she's on the edge of losing it. Tense like she's about to *explode*. It doesn't happen very often with my control-freak mother, but I have seen it when she's been frustrated about things going *mega* wrong at work, or being driven *mad* by Nana's contrariness, or the couple of times I've forgotten to phone her when I've been late home from Bella's or Aisha's and she's imagined I'm dead in a ditch. . .

"Should we get out of here? Go back to Nana's or something?" I suggest.

"Yes, yes! Good idea," Mum says, looking at me gratefully. "We've all got lots to talk about, so let's go somewhere more comfortable."

"*Not* Nana's, then!" I can't help but joke, even if it's the wrong time for goofing around.

Dean and Zephyr laugh; not that I care. But I'm relieved to see Mum manage a wry smile.

"Well, we've got satnav in the hire car," Dean says to Mum, as we all start readying ourselves to go. "So we'll meet you at Patsy's, then?"

"Yes, sure," Mum says curtly. "See you there in—"

Mum's mobile jangles to life in her bag. The ringtone is frantic – one she chose specially for anyone calling from the office.

"Sorry, I just have to take this," she says, grabbing her phone and purposefully walking away from us for a little privacy.

And now I'm left, stranded and shuffling, with Dean and Zephyr.

"It's her work," I mumble, just for something to say.

"Ah, yes." Dean nods. "Patsy says she does online ... office..."

"...innovation," I finish, and hope he doesn't ask what that means. "What, er, do *you* do?"

"I make eco log cabins back home in Australia. That's why I was in Cornwall; there was a big convention – all about different building materials."

"Basically, just different *logs*, then," I say, and then wish I hadn't. I can't help myself with the cheeky remarks sometime, but I should keep them for people I actually know. Though even the people I know don't find my comments too funny, sometimes. (Mum, mostly. And I drive Bella and Aisha mad with them sometimes.)

"Ha!" laughs Dean. "Got your sense of humour from your grandmother, I see!"

OK, now I'm blushing, *and* a little bit pleased. Nana always has been funny. I hadn't thought that—

Wait ... my backpack!

"I forgot my bag – it's by Nana's bed," I say hurriedly. "Can you tell Mum I've gone to get it?"

With that I grab hold of the sketchbook and my phone and hurry away, the rubber soles of my

Converse whacking on the vinyl flooring of the hospital corridors as I run.

WHACK! WHACK! The blood pumps through my frazzled brain, sharpening it into focus for the first time in hours.

WHACK! WHACK! What's going to happen to Nana if she has dementia?

WHACK! WHACK! Will she have to move into a home?

WHACK! WHACK! Or come and live with *us* in Chelmsford?

I slow as I clatter through the ward door, realizing I can't bear to think of Nana going into a home, but knowing for sure that having her in our little two-bedroom flat isn't going to be an option.

And most of all, I realize that I *don't* want the dementia diagnosis to be true...

"Hello," I say softly as I reach Nana's bed.

She's still sleeping, but I bend over and gently fasten the loose hair clip I spotted earlier, then plant a kiss on her downy cheek.

"Thank you for giving me Chapter Two of *The Pearl in the Attic*, Nana," I whisper. "It's perfect. I can't wait to read Chapter Three."

The heavy lids of her eyes may be shut, but I suddenly see Nana give a pleased little smile.

"You know, there's no smoke without a fire, Scarlet. . ." I hear her murmur.

"What?" I ask, feeling a chill of confusion. Is Nana rambling? Is this part of her condition?

"*You* heard, Scarlet," she says softly. "Kick-start those brain cells!"

And then her smile slips away into sleep again.

I straighten up, still staring at her.

And then a flicker of memory comes to me.

"Kick-start those brain cells!" That was what Nana used to say whenever I got stuck on clues she'd give during the fun paper trails around her garden.

This tells the time, but not at night led me to the sundial.

These bells will never ring took me to the patch of bluebells.

A secret passage! got me bending down at the fence with the broken chunk of panelling at the bottom where next door's cat liked to sneak through.

Hold on; Nana really *is* playing a game with me, isn't she?

Has she just given me a clue for Chapter Three?

No smoke without a fire. . .

"OK, Nana; understood," I whisper, feeling as if she's just presented me with a gift, in the mess and the muddle of everything.

Gathering up my bag, I speed away, now desperate to get back to the flat, whether we have our unexpected visitors or not.

And on the way there, I need to engage my eight-year-old clue-solving brain. . .

The Pearl in the Attic

Chapter 3

The full moon made silhouettes of the chimney pots.

Outside in the yard, the bakery building sat hunkered in the cool shadows, quiet and closed.

The windows of the houses beyond were mostly dark, with only the occasional flicker of a candle or the glow of gaslight to be seen.

Ruby held her own candle aloft, turned away from the window and surveyed the room she had been given. The furnishings – a bed, a chair, a table with a washbowl and jug, a cupboard – were plain and good. Yellow roses twined their way prettily up and down the wallpaper.

She might have considered herself very lucky, if she did not miss her family in Kent so dreadfully, and was not so dreadfully worried about the "family" she had come to in London.

Still, it was just the first day, she tried to tell herself, biting at her lip.

I'm fourteen now, and must be brave and make the best of—

Ruby froze at the sudden sound of the crashing and thrashing, and quickly blew out the candle she was holding.

It was as if a bear were loose on the stairs.

A bear disturbed from its hibernation, coming in search of the fool that had dared to awaken him.

"Gertie! GERTIE!" she heard her uncle bellow, his footfall a staggered thud on every tread, his big body crashing against wall and banister.

As he reached the landing and unevenly stamped his way towards the front bedroom, Ruby felt the tremor of every thumping step vibrate on the soles of her own bare feet.

SLAM!

At the bone-rattling sound of a door thrust shut, Ruby pressed her back against the glass of the window, wishing she could slip clean through it and disappear into the cool of the night air.

But perhaps all would be well. Perhaps her

uncle's evening on the ale would mean he'd collapse, drunkenly sleeping through till the early hours when he'd need to be up making the day's bread fresh for his customers.

Or perhaps not.

Muffled roars and cursing suddenly burst and buzzed through the wall.

"D'you HEAR me, woman!"

Fear fuelling her, Ruby rushed towards the shape in the shadows she knew to be the bed, planted the candlestick on the chair beside her and quickly crawled under the shelter of the scratchy blankets and worn counterpane.

". . .you will NOT disobey me. . ."

Lying in a rigid curl in the unfamiliar bed, Ruby tried to imagine the crowded, warm comfort of her wriggling little sisters about her ... but like a creeping fog, the noise of her uncle's foul temper – words marred and muddled by the slur of strong liquor – seemed to seep under her bedroom door and seek her out.

"Do you understand, you half-witted. . ."

On and on he yelled and hectored, yet the only response to Uncle Arthur's thundering was silence. What was happening in the room next door, Ruby fretted? Was Gertrude standing in her tall, dignified solitude, fixing her blank look upon her husband as he raged? Or was she cowering in her bed as Ruby was, wishing for but knowing there was no one at all to rescue her?

And then more sounds came which turned Ruby's skin clammy with fright – clatterings and thumps, as if someone had fallen or been thrown to the floor. Then one long, low groan.

Ruby barely breathed; a clock somewhere ticked, long minutes passing.

The quiet was not to be trusted, she felt. What did it mean? What secrets did it hold?

Tick-tock, tick-tock, tick-tock...

Another sound began to drone in the distance: snoring.

And another joined it: a shuffle, followed by a tap-tap, then scrabbling.

Ruby peeked out from under the covers and stared straight up at the source of these new noises – the ceiling.

The creature, or creatures, responsible were surely bigger than the mice she was so used to catching and shooing from the cottage back home.

Rats, perhaps?

At the thought of them, Ruby sunk further beneath her blankets, silently thankful that her aunt had not followed her husband's orders and given Ruby the attic as her lodgings.

Now a creak of a nearby door made Ruby shuffle up on to her elbows. Soft, slow footsteps this time. Footsteps that were not her uncle's.

Some twist turned in Ruby's stomach, and she thought of her mother, constantly lashed and belittled by Father's tongue. Aunt Gertrude may not have been warm to her in any way so far, but Ruby felt a rush of pity for this woman who plainly had to bear harsh blows as well as harsh words.

Without thinking, Ruby threw off the covers and ran to her own door, pulling it open. What comfort she might offer, she did not stop to think.

But Ruby's good intentions quickly evaporated, like the trailing smoke of a snuffed flame.

"What do you think you're doing?" hissed Aunt Gertrude, her hair now hanging down across the chest of her nightgown in a long plait like a great brown snake. It might have been a shadow cast by the candle she held, but it seemed to Ruby as if there was a livid red mark across the left-hand side of her aunt's face.

"I couldn't sleep because..." Ruby began, then halted.

Something in Aunt Gertrude's stare seemed to defy her to say the truth of what she had heard, Ruby realized. Perhaps the older woman thought it was not Ruby's place to draw attention to the matter, or perhaps her aunt could not face the shame of what had just occurred?

"...I heard some noises from the attic," Ruby continued instead.

"There's a window broken up there," Aunt Gertrude replied briskly. "Probably a pigeon's got in and can't find its way out again. I'll take a look tomorrow. Now get to bed – the morning will come soon enough."

Ruby closed the door softly on her aunt, and her intention to help.

She crawled back under the covers, not supposing for an instant that the sweet escape of sleep would come to her in this disquieting place...

The smell of alcohol spread like a mist, souring the sweet, sugary scent of the newly opened shop.

"Here," grunted Uncle Arthur, clattering a wooden tray of fancy bread rolls down on the table by the back door.

Ruby watched as he shot a look of what bordered on hatred at Aunt Gertrude, who ignored him and carried on sorting coins from the drawer of the imposing cash register for the shop's first customer of the morning.

Aunt Gertrude was using her right hand for this purpose, Ruby noticed. The left was pressed against her ribs, as if something there was causing pain.

Her own hands clutched across her chest, Ruby picked agitatedly at the skin around her nail, and wished that her uncle might leave, and return to the bakery in the yard. Even just a minute in his presence was no pleasure.

"And what are *you* staring at, missy!" he suddenly bellowed at Ruby.

His eyes: they were as familiar as Father's, but the dark, hard stare was far more fierce, far more threatening, and cut her to the core.

"Nothing, sir," Ruby said quickly, feeling herself shrink.

"Nothing, eh?" snarled Uncle Arthur, taking a menacing step towards her.

Without saying a word, Aunt Gertrude turned to face him, blocking his way and his view of Ruby.

Cowering behind her, Ruby held her breath, waiting for what might come next.

The looks exchanged between husband and wife she could not be sure of, but – thankfully – Uncle Arthur seemed to think better of whatever he had been of a mind to do.

"Out of my way!" he brayed, and Ruby heard him stamp off.

Peeking around her aunt, she saw Uncle Arthur walk through into the storeroom. Like some tyrant king of ancient times, he barged past old Mrs Price – the charwoman Ruby had recently been introduced to – as she stood aside in the shadows, broom in hand and head dutifully down.

As soon as her uncle's voice was heard booming back out in the yard – shouting at either Billy the delivery lad or Wilfred in the bakery – the mood in the front shop lightened a little, as if some lead-lined shawl had been lifted from the shoulders of Aunt Gertrude. The brightness was compounded by the tinkle of the bell above the door as the customer left, and Nell – putting a basket of fat, glazed buns in the window – suddenly burst out laughing.

"Will you look at that?" she said, turning to Aunt Gertrude and Ruby.

She was pointing out into the street. There were plenty of folk already about and strolling for their shopping in the high street, but now they were all slowing as something caught their gaze.

Aunt Gertrude lifted her skirts and swished forward, looking to join Nell, who was now opening the door. Even old Mrs Price had abandoned her cleaning as curiosity got the better of her.

Ruby was meant to be receiving instruction from her aunt this morning. So far she'd learned what Madeira tarts, fondant icing, kaiser rolls, desiccated coconut and candied angelica looked like. She'd discovered that a certain type of long, iced cake had three shades of sponge inside as you cut it and was known as a "masked genoise", and that the flaky cones of buttercream pastries were made from rolled, flat biscuits known as "langue de chat", or cat's tongues for those who did not understand French, which was most customers who came through the door, Ruby supposed. At least they would know no better if she pronounced them terribly.

And because she was afraid to leave her aunt's side, Ruby followed the three women out on to the pavement just as the most extraordinary gentleman rode by on his neatly trotting horse, waving a flag of stars and stripes on a pole.

"That's the flag of the United States of America!"

Ruby heard a mother tell her little son as she lifted him high in her arms.

As for the man, Ruby had only seen his likeness briefly yesterday – on the handbill the girl in the knickerbockers had tried to present to her – but she recognized this Wild West showman straightaway.

"What is this?" Aunt Gertrude asked, stretching her tall self even taller to take in the spectacle above the heads of the men and women now stopped on the pavements to do likewise.

"It's a show that's come to Ally Pally, Mrs Wells!" said Nell. "That's Colonel Samuel Cody, that is, and his troupe will perform a melodrama, my Fred says, about brave folk that were pioneers in America."

"*And* there's displays of bareback riding and a shooting show," Billy called out, joining in with the chatter as he pushed his laden bicycle out of the alleyway. "There's even a girl that floats clean into the sky on a balloon!"

Explanations given, Nell and Billy both pushed forward, the better to see the extravagantly bearded gentleman, while voices now roared from around him, alerting the crowds to the wonders they'd see if they come up to the palace.

"Fine-looking man, eh, Gertrude?" Ruby heard

Mrs Price say to her aunt, and spotted the twinkle in the older woman's eyes. "Looks quite the hero."

"Quite," replied Aunt Gertrude.

"Pity you couldn't just take that pearl from the attic, jump on the back of the stallion, and let Colonel Whatsisname carry you off to the prairies and away from here...!"

"*Shush*," Aunt Gertrude hissed at Mrs Price, and smartly turned to go back inside, nearly walking directly into Ruby.

"Sorry," said Ruby, pressing herself as small as she could against the shop doorway, her mind floundering between the unexpected excitement of seeing the showman close up, and the peculiar thing she'd overheard Mrs Price just say. Aunt Gertrude had some kind of *jewel* hidden upstairs?

For a moment, Ruby pictured a beautiful ring, a family heirloom, tucked into a crevice in the roof timbers, where Uncle Arthur would not find it...

"Come along – you must learn to use the cash register," Aunt Gertrude announced sharply to her.

At the mention of it, Ruby's heart sank at the thought of the gold-and-black beast with the pistons and pads with numbers she would struggle to make out, but dutifully followed her aunt nonetheless.

"Here," said Aunt Gertrude, taking something out of her white apron pocket.

She presented the item to Ruby, who took a moment to realize that the folded wires and rounds of glass were a pair of spectacles.

"They may not suit your eyes, of course, but try them and see," said Aunt Gertrude.

Ruby could not understand her aunt at all. The expression on her face was as unwelcoming as it had been from the first moment she had stared at Ruby through the shop window. Yet here she was, presenting her with spectacles that must surely have cost a pretty penny?

As if Aunt Gertrude could read Ruby's mind, she added in a flat tone, "They were my sister Irma's."

Mrs Price, passing behind Aunt Gertrude, cast a certain look in the direction of Ruby, one that clearly spoke of sadness. So the reason for this Irma no longer being in need of her spectacles was surely not a happy one...

Ruby took her hands from her chest where they had been so tightly clutched and reached for the offered gift. With trembling fingers she put them to her face, hooking the cold metal arms behind each ear.

"Well?" demanded Aunt Gertrude.

Taking a wary step forward, Ruby found herself directly in front of the cash register.

To her delight, each of the numbers was a hard, firm shape that could not fool her or muddle her.

"Yes ... I can see quite clear!" said Ruby. "Everything is so—"

"Oh, dear, no!" exclaimed Aunt Gertrude.

At first, Ruby presumed that something must be amiss with the way of her wearing the spectacles, and then she saw that her aunt was staring at the bib of Ruby's apron.

She dipped her head to see what had caused her aunt such distress, and beheld a thruppenny-sized mark of fresh blood on the snow-white starched cloth.

Aunt Gertrude grabbed at Ruby's hands, turning them this way and that as she studied the ragged soreness of the nails.

"This must stop," she barked. "You cannot serve customers looking like this! And you certainly cannot wear a bloodied apron. Go to your room and change into a fresh one straightaway. There's one folded in the cupboard."

Feeling her face hot with embarrassment, Ruby snatched her hands away, only to have to lift one again to take the key that Aunt Gertrude had unfastened from the ring at her waist and was holding out to her.

Giving a little bob, Ruby hurried out of the shop door – pausing only to let Nell come back in from the street – and quickly let herself into the flat above.

The shame coursing through her veins put a spring in Ruby's step, and she took the two staircases in no time at all, arriving breathless at her bedroom on the second floor.

In a panic, she flung off the offending apron, wondering how she might get it clean for tomorrow. She could perhaps ask Mrs Price if there was somewhere she could soak it, Ruby thought, as she quickly found the other apron and began fastening about her.

And then she heard it. . .

The scrape and tap of the bird – the pigeon? – in the attic directly above.

Ruby's fingers slowed in their knotting and her gaze fixed upon the ceiling.

What if it was trapped up there, as Aunt Gertrude had supposed?

Ruby thought of her mother's tears the day a sparrow had flown into the cottage by way of the open front door, its tiny body bashing against the walls as it struggled to be free, and panicked by Mother's attempts to drive it outside. It had fallen to the floor and breathed its last, and Mother was inconsolable as she took its limp body in her hands.

Ruby knew she was expected downstairs directly, but also remembered her aunt saying that she would deal with the bird today. If she quickly hurried upstairs now, Ruby could free the creature – or at least push open further the window it came through, so that it might fly out – and save her aunt the trouble.

Even though there was not a soul to disturb in the empty quiet of the two floors of the flat, Ruby made but the lightest step on the small staircase that led up to the attic.

As she did so, a thought came to her … the treasure mentioned by old Mrs Price – was there more? Other precious, sentimental gifts from Aunt Gertrude's first husband, Mr Brandt, maybe? All bundled out of sight of Uncle Arthur, who might otherwise claim them, then sell them and drink away the proceeds…

And of course, hidden pearls and jewels might be the *real* reason Aunt Gertrude risked defying her husband and resisted placing Ruby there. Why on earth would she trust a child she'd never met before, and one who happened to be a relative of Uncle Arthur's too?

Bristling and wishing she was no kin to her uncle at all, Ruby silently vowed that she would not go looking for nooks in rafters and loose floorboards. She was here to free the trapped creature, and that was all.

Now at the top landing, she came to door, unpainted and of poorer quality than the fine doors downstairs with their panels and trims.

Ruby took a quick, deep breath to steady herself for the task ahead.

Then found she could not breathe at all.

Through a long, vertical crack in the wood of the door, a wide blue eye stared at Ruby and blinked twice.

It seemed there was not a bird trapped inside.

And there was no ring-mounted gem hidden inside.

"Who's there?" Ruby whispered, though she already guessed the answer.

"Pearl," said the soft, scared voice of the girl...

How to Know It All – Or Not Quite

My head is jangling with what I've just read.

All this time, Pearl was a *girl*.

A sad, scared, hidden girl.

And thanks to Nana's beautiful writing, she's a girl who feels as alive to me right now as the people here in the living room.

I'm *desperate* to find out who she is and what happens next in Nana's story. But instead I have to play nice and perform waitress duties.

"Well, well, well. . ."

Angie bobs merrily along the back of the sofa where Mum and "Uncle" Dean are sitting, Mum uptight and perched on the edge of her seat, Dean comfortably sprawled back on a cushion mountain.

"Couldn't have said it better myself, Angie!" Dean says to the parrot with an easy laugh.

I hover with a tray of mugs and glasses, uncertain where to put it down. It's hard to know where to put *anything* down in the majority of Nana's flat. When I popped to the supermarket a couple of minutes ago to grab some orange juice and milk, I left Dean and Zephyr lifting bags and boxes off the sofas so that we could all have somewhere to sit together. (Mum was – of course – on the phone to her office.)

Boxes – that's it. With one foot, I carefully nudge a carrier bag stuffed with silky scarves off the nearest cardboard box, and plonk the mugs of tea and glasses of orange juice down on top of it.

At least I don't have to sit next to Zephyr on the other sofa; Mr Spinks has nabbed that spot and is lying on his back doing a doggy star-shape, pawing the air wildly while Zephyr tickles his pudgy tummy. A niggle of irritation crosses my chest at Mr Spinks's disloyalty...

Of course, what I'd *really* love to do is leave everyone here to it and disappear up to my room so I can reread Chapter Three of *The Pearl in the Attic*. It took a bit of finding at first; there's the chimney breast but no fireplace in my room. I almost gave up before I began, thinking I'd have to dig around in *all* the fireplaces in the flat. Then I had the idea to pull the futon away from the chimney-breast wall, and – blam! – there it was, the next packet of red-ribbon-wrapped papers neatly folded and slotted into a gap where a brick had worked loose.

I had to scan Nana's artfully scribbly writing pretty quickly – Dean and Zephyr showed up soon after Mum and I arrived back here from the hospital.

Mum had to shout at me to come down about three times; I kept looking at the ending of the chapter and then staring at the door of my room, imagining a frightened Pearl there, peering out at an equally startled Ruby...

When we visit Nana later, I'll have to thank her for the excellent clue and totally excellent chapter, and find a way of asking for the *next* clue without anyone hearing. After all, this more grown-up version of the paper-trail game is just *our* special thing, and that's how I want it to stay.

But hold on; Nana has her mobile by her bedside now... Maybe I should text her? Except (cue a grumble of guilt), I only got my new Nokia a couple of months ago and didn't think to put Nana's number in there, amongst my long list of school friends.

OK, so I'll get it from her later, for sure. In the meantime I could get back to Bella and Aisha – they got around the no-using-mobiles-in-school rule today by huddling together in a cubicle in the girls' loos at break time, where they messaged me, asking why I'm not in school.

How will I answer that, though? I was absent because we found out my grandmother's poorly, AND because we found out she has a secret. . .

1. dog
2. parrot
3. illness
4. hoarding habit
5. talent for writing
6. Australian family?

If I tried to text or message all that at once, my friends would probably suspect I'm fevered and delirious and babbling rubbish.

"Here," I say instead, at least remembering my manners as I pass tea to Mum and Dean, and orange juice to Zephyr.

I sit myself down in Nana's armchair and plonk the remaining cup on the small table next to it, keeping my own glass of orange juice in my hand.

Right on cue, Angie flutters on down and dips her beak in the cup of lukewarm tea I made her specially. (Milk, no sugar, I guessed.)

"Ha! That is SO funny seeing her do it for real!" Zephyr says with a big grin as he wrestles his mobile out of his pocket. "I mean, Patsy showed us on Skype already, but this is so cool!"

Another ripple of irritation crosses my chest. Does Zephyr and his dad know *everything* there is to know about Nana's life, right down to the tea-drinking habits of her pets?

As Zephyr sets about filming Angie in slurping action – tilting her head back to let the tea trickle down her throat – I glance over at the mantelpiece that's packed with framed photos and ornaments, all jostling for space. And there's the photo of an older, dark-haired bloke (Grandad Manny) holding the baby version of the surfer boy on the sofa across from me. At least Nana has a picture of me up there too. Pity it's a school photo aged seven with more gaps in my smile than actual *teeth*...

"Weird creature," Mum mutters, staring at Angie.

"Who knows how my mother ended up with it!"

"Oh, don't you know the story?" asks Dean. "Seems Angie escaped from somewhere, or more likely was deliberately let loose in the park around Ally Pally."

My uncle must notice me and Mum frowning.

"Ally Pally? It's the nickname of Alexandra Palace, the big iconic building near here?" Dean explains.

"Oh, yeah – of *course* we know Alexandra Palace!" I say quickly, even though the closest I've come to it is in Nana's story. "I was going to take Mr Spinks for a walk there over the weekend."

Once I google it and find out where it is exactly. . .

"Great! I'll come!" says Zephyr.

I don't say anything back. There's a second's awkward pause, and then Dean starts up his Angie tale again.

"Well, talking of walking Mr Spinks, Patsy was in Ally Pally Park with him one day and came across Angie on the grass, getting mobbed by a bunch of crows. Patsy threw her jacket over her, bundled her up and took Angie back here. She tried to find her owner. Put up flyers locally and posted on websites, but no one came forward."

"And the dog?" Mum asks, since Dean apparently has all the answers.

"Tied up outside the supermarket downstairs," Zephyr chips in as he lowers his phone. "Mr Spinks was there all day, so Patsy guessed he'd been dumped and took him in. She told the security guard and the shop manager, just in case anyone had, you know, accidentally forgotten their dog for eight hours..."

OK, so I forgive Mr Spinks for allowing Zephyr to stroke him after knowing him for exactly half a second. How could anyone abandon such a cute-ugly dog? To let him sit there on the pavement, alone and hungry, his pleading amber eyes watching everyone go by, hour after ticking hour? And Angie, tippetty-tappitting from clawed foot to clawed foot in happiness right now as she has her special treat of Tetley's ... to think of her lost and bewildered in the wild, being used as pecking practice for a bunch of thuggish crows.

They were *so* lucky to be found by my lovely nana.

A tug in my tummy makes me think of my gran again now.

Did Nana feel abandoned by Mum and me over the last year? I wonder. Did she look at my photo on the mantelpiece and miss the chats and fun we used to have when I was younger?

And when me and Mum go back to Chelmsford, will Nana feel lost and bewildered – with only a fat dog and crazy parrot for company – as the quicksand of dementia starts to suck her into a different, unrecognizable world....?

"What can we do to help Nana?" I blurt out, my jealousy over Dean and Zephyr's closeness to Nana on pause now that genuine worry has taken over.

"Right," says Mum, slapping her hands on her knees, and looking instantly less uncomfortable now that she's switching into Practical Mode. "Zephyr, I'm sure your dad talked to you on the way over here, and told you what was discussed in the meeting at the hospital."

Zephyr nods. So he's heard what I have: that they'll keep Nana in under observation over the weekend. That on Monday some specialist person will do some test on Nana, asking her a bunch of questions to find out where her head's at (quite literally). That a social worker needs to visit the flat on Monday, to check if it's possible for Nana to come back here and be safe and comfortable. Ha ha ha ha...

"Obviously, we need to do a massive clean-up and clear-out here," Mum carries on, staring around and probably wishing she had a clipboard so she could make a to-do list and assign us all tasks.

"Well, we're here, and ready to dive in!" says Dean.

"Great," Mum replies with a nod. "So I've already googled and found a rubbish dump nearby with weekend opening hours. We just have to decide whether we want to hire a van so we can get rid of all this junk quickly, or just do several trips in the two cars."

"Whoa!" exclaims Zephyr. "We can't just *dump* it all! Patsy spent ages getting all this stuff together. She was going to open up, like, some vintage store downstairs."

"Zeph's right; it was what she was hoping to do," Dean chips in, nodding sagely, though Mum is rolling her eyes at the sound of *another* Nana plan. "She was only storing things here in the flat till she found someone to do building work and decorate downstairs."

"But it's all total trash!" Mum says, frowning as she waves her hands around at the assorted boxed and bagged stuff-ness.

Actually, I hate to side with my unknown uncle and cousin, but I kind of *do* think some of this junk is cool, and some of it *might* be valuable. I'm sure I've seen ancient 1960s phones – like the ones on the cabinet here – in the style section of magazines. The old, fancy flowery teapots that line the small staircase to the loft; they look like they may be worth something. And when we were on our way to the hospital, I saw a couple of vintage clothes shops that would surely be interested in buying some of the second-hand coats and dresses and shoes Nana's collected. (Not before *I've* gone through them first, though...)

"Hey, maybe we could store it all down in the shop for now, so the flat's not such a mess," I suggest. "Then Nana can decide what to do with it later, once she's back home...?"

Dean and Zephyr nod at my idea, but Mum is giving me the glare of doom. I guess her neat-freak side had clearly been looking forward to sweeping the flat clean in one satisfying fell swoop.

"Fine," she says wearily, "but we'll have to find the keys for downstairs first. I had a look around in all the drawers this morning, but no luck. And where do you even start in a mess like this? It'll be like looking for a needle in a haystack."

"Hmm, well, we can ask Patsy when we visit

later, of course," says Dean, "but it would be good to get started clearing this straightaway, really, since there's so much—"

Dean's suggestion is interrupted by Mum's mobile jangling with an incoming text.

"Sorry," Mum apologizes, rifling for the phone in her bag on the floor. "I've got to check this in case it's something important to do with work. Oh; actually, it's a text from my mother. Her ears must've been burning!"

"Is Patsy all right?" Dean asks, before I have the chance to.

"Uh-uh," Mum mutters distractedly, as she reads what's written on the small screen. "She's given me a description of the pyjamas she wants; I chose the wrong ones earlier, apparently. Zephyr, she's asking if you can show her how to use FaceTime when you visit so she can chat to Angie and Mr Spinks later on. Oh, and this is for you, Scarlet. She says to tell you, *number four is all in a day's work*... Does that make any sense?"

I feel Mum, Dean and Zephyr's questioning eyes on me.

"Mmm, sort of," I answer non-committally, though I'm buzzing inside at the thought of another clue in my chapter hunt. Even if I don't have the faintest idea yet what it means.

I'm just about to ask Mum if I can have her phone to text Nana back when the stupid thing blasts out that annoyingly frantic ringtone that *definitely* means the office is calling.

"Sorry. Excuse me," she mutters, jumping to her feet and clip-clopping out of the room in her smart work shoes.

"Actually," says Dean, getting to his feet too, "I'm going to go up to our room, Zeph. It's nearly midnight back home in Melbourne, but hopefully your mum's still awake and I can quickly let her know what's happening."

"OK," Zephyr mutters, holding his phone up in front of him again as he films Mr Spinks's fat tummy and then swoops around, taking in the wonders of the over-stuffed living room. I lean out of the way, in case he's trying to get *me* in there.

Angie doesn't seem keen on getting in the shot either, and hops off the table and on to the arm of my chair. Us camera-shy girls are sticking together.

"Love the one of the Rose Window," Zephyr says, now aiming the phone at the three paintings on the back wall.

"The what?" I say, though Zephyr *has* to be talking about the third picture, the one of a circle of stained glass in a triangular brick wall.

"The Rose Window...?" he says, turning back to me with an I-can't believe-you-don't-know-that expression. "It's, like, the *main* feature of Alexandra Palace. You can see it from the attic."

Aargh! How does this boy from the other side of the world know so much more than I do, including the view from my own bedroom here?

I'm about to get up from my seat and go upstairs to unpin the makeshift tea-towel curtain when Zephyr carries on yakking.

"Cool story about Nana proposing to Grandad Manny right under the Rose Window, isn't it?"

Angie is weaving and bobbing on the arm of the chair, which is a bit distracting. But I still manage to spot Zephyr throw me the quickest of sideways glances. He knows I have no clue about this, doesn't he? Same as I don't know a ton of other Nana-related details that *he* clearly does.

I'm going to have to fake it.

"I can totally picture Nana just going for it," I say as Angie continues to dip and dive, as if she's examining my hair.

141

"Grandad always said Patsy was like a whirlwind," says Zephyr, lowering the phone and turning back to me. "He knew as soon as he met her in the café that she was pretty special."

Time for more faking.

"Which café was it again?" I ask, trying to pull away the lilac lock of hair that Angie is experimentally tugging at with her beak.

"One that was near her art college," says Zephyr, as Mr Spinks lazily paws at him upside down, desperate for more tummy tickles. "Grandad Manny went in there, when he was visiting his sister Sita. Isn't it weird that she was doing her nursing training at the same hospital Patsy's in now?"

OK, I've given up on faking.

I must look ridiculous. My mouth is hanging open in surprise and I'm trying to restrain a parrot from eating my hair.

So my middle name *isn't* some random, pretty Indian name from a random member of the Chaudhary clan, but an actual great-aunt who used to live around here?

My family – it's getting bigger and more complicated by the minute...

Though I can't quite concentrate on the latest

mind-tangling piece of news, since the hair-tugging is getting quite sore and irritating and I have no idea how to discipline a bird.

"Stop it!" I say, flailing my arms around, sending my glass of orange juice tumbling to the floor.

"WHEEEEEEEEEEEP!" comes a loud whistle, and I feel Angie release my hair and hear her flap, flap off.

There's a *TINK, TINKLE, TINK!* followed by a clipping noise. I shove my hair off my face just in time to see Zephyr closing the door to Angie's cage.

"I've seen Patsy do the whistling thing on Skype – when Angie's getting too playful and needs time out in there," he says.

Great. Zephyr knows everything about absolutely *everything* around here, including how to train an African grey parrot.

Or maybe he doesn't know *quite* everything.

As the chunky glass spins stickily to a stop at my feet, a spark of memory pops into my head. The jar Nana always kept hidden behind the hydrangea bush at her old house, spare keys dry and safe inside.

"Where are you going?" asks Zephyr as I leap up and run out into the hall.

"I think I might know how to find the keys to the shop," I mutter, not caring if he can hear me or not.

There's a sudden skitter of claws on the floor as Mr Spinks runs alongside me, probably assuming that he's about to get another walk. As I open the door at the top of the stairwell, he nimbly dashes down the stairs to the front door without sending even one of the dozens and dozens of books flying.

And it's one particular stack of books that I'm interested in.

There, at the bottom, opposite the Harry Potters, is a pile of gardening books. One large one is leaning up against the wall, an image of a blue-mauve mass of flowers on it. A hydrangea bush. Mr Spinks thuds his tail on the ground and pants happily as I crouch down beside him and lift the book towards me, away from the wall.

"Yessss!" I call out, reaching out for the glass jar that's hidden behind it.

"Yes, what?" asks Zephyr, padding down the stairs in time to see me holding up the jar and rattling the two sets of keys inside.

I twist off the lid and reach inside.

"Think these are spares for the front door here," I tell him, the ordinary set jangling in my hand against a darker, chunkier pair of keys, "and the others are for the shop!"

"I'll tell Dad! And Aunt Ren!" Zephyr announces, hurtling back up the stairs.

But I'm not about to wait for any of them.

"Stay!" I order Mr Spinks as I open the front door, pushing the disappointed dog gently back inside with my leg.

And just a few seconds after clunking one door shut behind me, I'm unlocking and shoving another one open.

The reason for the shoving is obvious as soon as I get inside the musty shop – piles of junk mail sit behind it. But Nana must have been in fairly recently; a neater pile of junk mail has been placed up on top of one of the three counters arranged around the room.

"Three counters," I murmur, and then look at the old-fashioned dark wooden shelves that line the walls, and the closed door at the back that must lead through to a storeroom of sorts, and the yard beyond.

No wonder Nana was inspired to set her story here, I think as I slowly walk around the counters, stopping where I assume a till would sit, if this was a bustling, busy baker's shop. Nothing has been changed in here for decades, except for the fact that there are strip lights in the ceiling, I notice, instead of gaslights hissing.

I stand for a moment, watching dust motes swirl in the little shafts of sunshine managing to peek through between the fly-posters gumming up the large front window.

I try to imagine Ruby standing here on that first day, surrounded by counters filled to the brim with coloured and creamed cakes and biscuits, instead of dead, dried-up flies and what look like old paper bags.

And then something hits me. Did Nana *really* just make up her tale of *The Pearl in the Attic* because she'd been inspired by the shop as a setting? Or is it based on a true story?

I mean, was Ruby *real*?

And Pearl. . . ?

Prickles of excitement and possibility make the hairs on my arms rise up.

And then something *else* hits me.

Standing here, serving customers . . . it would be all in a day's work for Ruby, wouldn't it?

All in a day's work. . .

My eyes dart madly around the mostly empty shop, then settle on the glass-topped counter where my hands are resting.

You know, those aren't old paper bags inside the counter.

They're sheets of cream paper, folded and tied with a dark red ribbon. . .

The Pearl in the Attic

Chapter 4

A latch scraped back, and the door was pulled open.

She was skinny, the girl who stood warily, just inside the room. Her eyes seemed huge in her gaunt, milk-white face.

And there was a strange softness to her person: a haze around her, as if she were an apparition, almost. . .

Just as Ruby felt a kick of panic in her belly, she realized the cause of the softness was the spectacles she was wearing, which were only for reading and close work.

With trembling fingers, she unhooked them, folded them neatly and slipped them into her apron pocket.

Now she could see the girl more clearly. Her red hair was scraped back into a messy bun, and seemed in need of washing. The white pinafore she wore over some grey clothing was clean enough, though. And she wore woollen stockings, but no boots or shoes.

Were they of around the same age, Ruby wondered? She thought so.

"Are you Ruby?" asked the girl, staring at Ruby as much as Ruby was staring at her.

"I. . . How do you know?" Ruby stumbled over her words.

"The only other girl or young woman here is Nell, I think," the girl replied. "And I do not suppose you are her. . ."

Pearl looked at Ruby's stomach and made a little round gesture with her hand over her own.

Ruby almost smiled – but then questions and wondering and worry took over again.

"Who are you?" she asked, looking back down the stairs, though no one was there.

"I'm Pearl. Come," said the girl, ushering her inside.

Ruby hesitated, taking only one step forward, enough to see what lay inside the attic.

And what she saw inside made her take a step more.

The sloping-roofed room was bare enough. But there were comforting touches too ... a paisley-patterned counterpane on a mattress that lay on the floor, a chair with a dainty oil lamp upon it, a cheerful rag rug, a posy of dried violets in an old jar, some books piled along the far wall where the chimney breast jutted out.

And papers ... paper *bags*, in fact they were, lay spread on an old wooden chest, with drawings scribbled upon them in charcoal.

Bags that were normally used downstairs in the shop, for the cakes and breads.

"What are you doing here?" Ruby asked, taking a further step inside, and seeing more signs of regular habitation. A tapestry bag with knitting needles sticking out. A dirty plate with a cup and a fork neatly piled upon it. A chamber pot in the corner.

"Living. Hiding," Pearl answered, clutching one arm with the other, and smiling shyly. "I heard you crying in the night."

Ruby's cheeks coloured a little. She had eventually sunk into the deep, dark sleep of exhaustion after her encounter with her aunt on the stairs last night, but woke herself up with muddled dreamings and sobs well before dawn.

"I heard you too," she told Pearl. "Just creaks and taps, as you moved about. I thought you were a rat."

"Oh, dear," Pearl giggled, baring her two front teeth, and lifting her hands to become claws.

Ruby really did giggle this time, then jumped back in fright as a great flapping commotion happened at a small window in one of the sloping walls.

"It's all right. It's my friend," said Pearl, reaching into the pocket of her pinafore for a few crumbs, which she held up to the bird that was now settling itself at the rim of the window.

As she waited for her breath to return, Ruby crept a little closer to the strange girl and the cooing bird.

"It keeps me company," said Pearl, smiling at first at the pigeon and then at Ruby. "It reminds me of the seagulls of home."

"Where is home?" Ruby asked, though the room around her seemed to be very much where Pearl was living.

"Hastings..." she replied, her smile fading. "Father died of a fever in the spring, and mother died a fortnight past. Tante Trudy came to the funeral. *He* did not come. *He* said under no circumstances was she to bring me back here, but she did."

Ruby didn't know where to begin: to say how

sorry she was to hear of such a loss, to ask who this Tante Trudy was, and who "*he*" was.

"Tante is German for aunt," explained Pearl, seeing Ruby's confusion. "She was my mother's sister."

"Irma!" exclaimed Ruby, her fingers touching the spectacles in her pockets.

So Tante Trudy was Auntie Gertrude. And of course, the "*he*" was Uncle Arthur. . .

"Yes!" Pearl smiled again. "Did Tante Trudy tell you?"

"She – she gave me these," Ruby said apologetically, pulling the spectacles a little way out of her pocket. "I hope you don't mind? Aunt Gertrude saw that I could not read my numbers, so. . ."

"Ah, she is so kind," said Pearl, her eyes pooling a little with tears.

"She does not care for *me* so very much," Ruby murmured, thinking of her aunt's blank looks and brusque manner.

"It's not your fault," said Pearl, dropping her gaze as she tried to find a few more crumbs in her pocket for the cooing, hungry bird. "Tante's husband refused to have me come here because he had already promised his brother he'd take *you*. He told her they could afford only one charity case, and that she should leave me to the poorhouse's care."

Pearl's words – Uncle *Arthur's* words – curdled in Ruby's stomach. He had used *Ruby* as a reason not to help a girl who was dreadfully in need. He thought of Ruby as a charity case, when she knew she would be made to work long hours for her keep, with no charity involved.

And most of all, she realized what this all meant.

"He does not know that you are here..." Ruby stated slowly.

Pearl lifted her head and shook it from side to side.

"Oh, my, no! He would beat Tante Trudy black and blue if he knew, I am certain!" said Pearl.

From the little she knew of him, Ruby was certain too. Which made Pearl's presence more concerning.

"Yet still, she risked that to bring you here," said Ruby.

"Yes..." Pearl replied, with a small, grateful smile. "Tante Trudy took me back here after Mother's funeral. She knew that she would; she had her friend Mrs Price help her set up this room beforehand. And by the time we arrived here from Hastings, it was late, and *he* was drunk and snoring on the sofa in the parlour."

"How … how do you manage?" Ruby asked, waving her hands around.

"Tante Trudy and Mrs Price bring me food, take my chamber pot away and fetch clean clothes. I would love a soak in a tin bath, though," Pearl said wistfully, sleeking a hand over her greasy hair. "But it is not for long. Tante Trudy will arrange something, I am sure of it."

"What sort of something?" Ruby asked.

"A position as a kitchen maid, perhaps. There are so many houses new built around here, Tante says," Pearl answered her. "I don't mind whether it is a grand place or quite small, as long as it is an occupation where I may live in."

Ruby began to bite at her lip. It would not be easy to get such a position in a house, however lowly it was, without a letter of good conduct – and the only person who could write such a letter for Pearl was Aunt Gertrude. This neighbourhood of Hornsey was unfamiliar to Ruby, but she imagined it like the village and outlying lands back home in Kent. How long would it take for word of Aunt Gertrude's recommendation to get back to Uncle Arthur. . . ?

"But for a short time, it is not so very bad here," Pearl said, putting a last few crumbs down for her feathered friend. "I read and draw, and I look at the view. Come see ... what do you suppose that is?"

Ruby took herself close enough to Pearl that they stood shoulder to shoulder, head tilted to head.

Through the open window, above the body of the contentedly pecking bird, she saw a sight that made her gasp. Alexandra Palace – where she had alighted at the station with Father yesterday – loomed above the rooftops in splendid isolation on its hill.

Ruby had not seen this view of it yesterday; her back had been to the building as she and Father stared at the far-off smoke trails of central London, and the bustling suburb of Hornsey that lay beneath them.

But now she saw it as it was meant to be seen ... a long, colonaded building with glass domes and towers at either end and a great, grand middle brick section that housed a vast, splendid circle of stained glass. At the apex of this brick section stood a figure: an angel, it seemed.

"It's Alexandra Palace," said Ruby, though she wondered why Pearl would not already know it, since she had been imprisoned here for the past two weeks. "Do you think King Edward stays there sometimes?"

She knew the new king lived mostly at Buckingham

Palace, like his late mother, Queen Victoria, before him.

"No – it was named after the king's wife, but it was built for the pleasure of ordinary folk, Tante Trudy told me," said Pearl. "It is known as the People's Palace. Tante Trudy went there to hear concerts with her husband, my uncle Karl. But I don't mean the palace; I'm talking of that large dome. . ."

What Pearl pointed to was a giant balloon, gently swaying in the wind, tethered in the grounds of the palace it seemed.

"There is a show and all manner of entertainments happening there," said Ruby, thinking of the girl with the handbills and the American gentleman on his steed. "The hot air balloon must be part of—"

Ruby's words were rudely interrupted by a tremendous roaring from outside. That, and the sound of shattering glass, sent Pearl's bird soaring into the sky, seeking the solace of its fellows.

"I'd better go," muttered Ruby, tingling ripples of fear in her chest, aware she had been gone from her post longer than she should have been.

But a thought struck her before she took her leave.

"Will you tell your aunt – *our* aunt – about this?" she asked, turning back at the doorway.

"No! Tante Trudy told me to stay hidden, to let no one but she and Mrs Price know that I am here, so that I'm safe. She might be angry with me for not keeping my promise," said Pearl. "But you won't... I mean, you won't tell, will you?"

Ruby looked at the gaunt girl with the pleading blue eyes. Yesterday, Ruby had felt herself to be frighteningly alone in this place, but here was someone in an even worse position. Of course she was not going to tell.

"Cross my heart and hope to die," she vowed, before swiftly closing the door behind her.

"Please come and see me again," she heard Pearl say plaintively, as she hurried away down the little staircase. "Please..."

The Snow Globe of Life

Twenty-four hours exactly.

When I took the call for Mum at our flat last night, the kitchen clock read 7.28.

And now, as we hurry along the hospital corridor this Friday evening, the hands of a nearby wall clock stand at the exact same time.

And it's been twenty-four hours where everything has changed. I mean, no one's died – except, I guess, a grandad I didn't know – but everything feels upside down and flung around.

Before the phone call from the hospital, it was as if me and Mum were in a little snow globe of our own, happily encased and ignoring each other in a nice calm scene . . . until some giant hand of fate grabbed the globe and shook it like it had a grudge against it.

When our globe-for-two was set back down, all these figures and flotsam and jetsam came snowstorming all around us.

Unexpected stuff like dogs, parrots, cousins and uncles.

Distressing stuff like clutter and worry and illness.

Wonderful stuff like rediscovering Nana, and losing myself in the long-ago world of Ruby and Pearl...

In fact, everything's *so* mad, I half expect my dad to float down by my side at any minute.

"You have GOT to be joking!" Mum growls at her mobile in her hand as if she hates it.

"What has that phone ever done to you?" I joke, trying to lighten the mood.

"The *phone* I like. My *boss*, I don't," says Mum, typing something quickly as she walks.

My DMs squeak on the polished floors as I pad along beside her. We're both in clean clothes – we drove home to Chelmsford this afternoon to get showered and pack enough things to last us a few days, as well as clean day-old cheesecake off the kitchen floor. Dean and Zephyr stayed at Nana's to start tidying, and were planning on visiting her this afternoon, while we were gone.

"So your *brother* said Nana was OK when they were here?" I ask, grinning sideways at Mum, trying out the word to see how she reacts to it.

"Yeah, the text from *Dean* said she was fine," Mum replies, rolling her eyes and obviously still struggling with the idea of Dean being her half-sibling. "And like I said in the car, Scarlet, I'm not exactly jumping for joy at having relatives come out of the woodwork. But to be honest, it's a bit of a godsend having Dean and Zephyr around to help out for a couple of days, with the mess of the flat and everything. . ."

Mum waves her hand in the air. Obviously, I get it that "everything" includes the worry over Nana and the inescapable pressure of work this week. Work was what stopped us talking about the weirdness of the day in the car; Mum kept having calls roll in on her Bluetooth, and so I'd ended up mostly zoning out with my headphones and fielding texts from Bella and Aisha, who were more interested in how cute my surprise cousin was than how Nana was doing.

Guess Mum was in the same boat. I heard her get quite a few "Sorry to hear that"s from her colleagues, but then when they realized Nana *wasn't* at death's door, it was back to them wondering when Mum would have the PowerPoint ready and did she know if the caterers at the convention were doing gluten-free options?

Mum's friend Nicki wouldn't win an Empathy Award anytime soon, either. Mum called her from the car, and I could hear Nicki make lots of "Oh, dear!" sorts of noises, before she started grilling Mum on where she got her cabin-sized suitcase because it would be *perfect* for her weekend away in Paris. . .

"And like I say, everything will be back to normal soon, Scarlet," Mum carries on. "We'll find out what's happening with Nana and get something sorted. Dean and Zephyr will go back to Australia. And it'll be just me and you again. OK?"

"OK," I reply, though I'm not sure how everything *can* get back to normal, if Nana isn't, well, ever going to be her normal self again.

And then I notice Mum's slowing down as we get closer to the double doors of Ward 9.

"Actually, hold on, Scarlet," Mum says, and I see

that her make-up might be fresh, but tiredness is still seeping through the mask of it. "We have to remember that we don't know how Nana will be. So if she's, you know, *different* any time we're visiting, then it's because of her condition. I just thought I'd say; I don't want you getting upset. All right?"

"Sure," I reply with a nod. Though I wonder if Mum is sort of reminding herself too.

Difficult as it is, Mum'll manage to do the PowerPoint over the weekend and *will* find out about gluten-free lunch choices. But it doesn't matter how competent and organized she is; Nana – and what's wrong with her – is something Mum can't fix.

For a second, I think about reaching out and giving her a hug, but then don't. I'm a little bit worried she might break.

"Right. Let's do this," she says, taking a deep breath and heading briskly for the ward doors.

I follow, and looking past the beds of propped-up patients, the nodding heads of concerned-but-smiling visitors, I see Nana. She's chatting to a nurse, who seems to be admiring a huge, fat bouquet of sunflowers on Nana's bedside table. I can practically feel the skinny bunch of flowers I picked up in the petrol station begin to wilt in my hand.

"Well, well, well!" Nana announces delightedly when she sees us. "Here's my daughter and granddaughter. At least *they're* easy to explain!"

"I was asking who the flowers were from. . ." the nurse begins.

". . .and I was telling her how difficult it is to describe who Dean and Zephyr are!" Nana jumps in.

Sigh. I *knew* the flowers were from them. I might as well put mine in the nearest bin.

"Well, *these* days, there are so many blended families, someone needs to invent a new batch of terms for everyone we love!" the nurse suggests as she drifts off and leaves us.

At that last chunk of her sentence, me and Mum swap looks, and the tiniest of smirks. I don't think Dean and Zephyr are ever going to fall into the category of people we love. More like people we'll tolerate for the next few days till they go back to Australia.

"Been watching something on your iPad, Nana?" I ask, trying to change the subject away from the two you-know-whos. The iPad is lying on the top of Nana's covers, and there's a picture of a stocky, imposing-looking building on the screen.

"Dean brought it from home earlier," Nana says,

and my heart sinks, since a conversation without a mention of my uncle and cousin seems impossible. "And Zephyr; what a sweetie he is. He looked up all these photos for me and made me a slide show. Look at this. . . Oh, you'll need to swipe for me."

Mum puts her hand out but Nana swivels the iPad around so it's facing more towards me. Maybe it hurts her to hold it in Mum's direction.

"So what's this?" I ask as we look at the building, with young women and men hovering outside, all with the long hair and flared trousers of the 1970s.

Mum has to lean over more, since the iPad is tilted slightly away from her.

"*That's* my old art college," says Nana. "And look what it is now. . ."

I swipe to a newer version of the building, and it's got a sign outside saying it's a primary school.

"And the next photo is of the café that I met Manny in. See what it is today? A hairdresser's!" Nana says excitedly. "And wait till you see *this* one . . . it's the old railway line that used to run up to Alexandra Palace. That was still there when I lived in the area, but all the rails have been taken up and it's now called the Parkland Walk. You can join it just up the road from here, and it takes you straight into the grounds of Alexandra Palace. It's a lovely walk – Mr Spinks and I have done it *lots* of times."

As Nana chatters on, I flick to a shot of overgrown greenery. At the same time I realize something. She's saying all of this to *me*, as if Mum's not there...

"And here're some views of Alexandra Palace itself," Nana carries on, as I swipe away. "Manny and I used to love sitting on the terrace, staring off at the skyline of London, making all our plans for the future."

That's it; I'm definitely going to go and explore the palace and park with Mr Spinks tomorrow.

"I didn't know that was such a special place for you and Dad. You've never mentioned it to me before," Mum says, reaching out to turn the iPad around a touch so that she can see the grand building properly.

Nana – surprisingly – yanks it away from her.

"Well, *here's* something I'll mention to you now," Nana says tetchily. "What's this nonsense about me having dementia?"

Now me and Mum exchange glances *minus* any smirks.

"So someone's talked to you about that?" Mum asks warily.

"Well, yes. A doctor who looked about twelve. I mean, bless him, but what does he know about *me*?" says Nana, wafting her good hand about in the air. "And I know that's what your meeting was about this morning. I hope you put them straight, Ren!"

So *that's* why Nana's been a bit funny with Mum. She's cross and upset and isn't sure that Mum has been standing up for her.

As for Mum, she's taken aback, it's obvious.

"Look, I'm not a medical expert," she replies to Nana quickly. "You seemed very confused when you came in here last night. The staff were a bit concerned."

"And I'm concerned that my own daughter didn't tell them how ridiculous the whole idea is!" says Nana. "Of *course* I was confused. *You* try sounding sensible when you've broken a bunch of bones and you're in agony!"

Mum opens her mouth and looks like she's struggling to say something in her defence – and then is saved by the bell. Or at least the ringtone of the office.

"It's my boss. I have to take it. I'll be quick," says Mum, looking like she might *love* instead of *hate* her demanding boss right at this second.

I knew what was going on: Mum would talk to her boss; then she'd take a slow, counting-to-ten breather before breezing back in here in Practical Mode, explaining to Nana crisply and clearly what was going to happen and why.

"Oh, your dear mother!" Nana sighs once Mum's out of earshot, giving me a weary smile. "I know I drive her mad. Always have done. But I was never a typical mum, and I'm not a typical 'old lady' and I don't want to be. I mean, *you* don't think there's anything wrong with me, do you, Scarlet, sweetheart?"

Nana's mischievous eyes twinkle as much as the pretty, glinting clips in her hair.

OK, so she was all over the place last night, smiling one minute and crying the next, but like she explained, she was in agony and on mega-strong painkillers.

But today, if I factor out my utter shock at meeting Dean and Zephyr, I can see that Nana's been fine. Tired but fine.

Speaking about Dean and Zephyr: I might not love their know-it-all take on all things Nana-centric, but they *have* explained why her flat looks like a madman's warehouse.

You know, suddenly, I really *do* think she's OK!

Happiness bubbles up inside me as I consider the possibility that the doctor last night jumped to conclusions and will be proved wrong.

It's *Nana* who's right.

They don't know how gorgeously eccentric and creative and fun she is. Nobody knows that better than me.

"Nana, I absolutely, one hundred per cent, don't think you have dementia," I tell her earnestly, clutching her good hand and earning a smile that's like the sun coming out.

"Oh, you are *so* like me, Scarlet," Nana says happily, casting her eyes over my lilac hair and the pink jacket I'm wearing over a T-shirt with a grinning yellow smiley face. "Your mum's different from us. She's never known how to have fun. She never takes chances on things! I mean, take your father, for example. Why she didn't just take off with him when she had the chance—"

"Sorry about that," says Mum matter-of-factly, hurrying back to rejoin us. "Now, where were we? Ah, yes ... the doctor. Look, all you need to do is take the test on Monday and if everything is fine, then—"

"Sorry, Ren," Nana takes a turn to interrupt, "but I'm on a lot of medication – *as you know* – and it's making me very sleepy. Can we talk about this tomorrow?"

Mum bats her kohl-edged eyes and clenches her jaw.

Nana shuts her eyes and shuts us out.

And me? My head is fizzing like it's packed with sherbet.

No one ever talks about my dad. Not Mum, not Nana, not me. He was never in my life, so I'm not supposed to miss him. But why has Nana brought him up now?

"Night, Scarlet," Nana mutters. "And don't forget to say goodnight to the palace for me. . ."

"I will. Night, Nana," I say, bending over to kiss her. "I'll get your number from Mum and text you a photo of it from my window tonight, OK?"

Nana doesn't reply, either because she's truly fast asleep or because she wants to block Mum.

And I can sort of see why. . .

"Well, your nana seems pretty out of sorts tonight," says Mum, as soon as we get through the ward doors and walk towards the lift.

"She's fine," I say sharply. "She just needs to know we're on her side, that's all."

"What do you mean?" Mum asks, shooting me a look.

"Listen, Nana says she doesn't have dementia, and I believe her, and *you* should too," I burst out at high speed. "I mean, she's written this brilliant story, and how could she do that if she was losing her mind? And the clues she's given me so I can find the chapters, that takes a *lot* of thinking about and—"

"Scarlet," Mum cuts in over me. "I don't want this to be true any more than you do. But we *have* to be realistic. If the hospital thinks there's a reasonable chance that—"

"Fine! Believe the hospital if you want!" I say, taking my turn to interrupt.

"Well, I seem to be *everyone's* favourite person tonight," Mum grumbles, tight-lipped.

I hear the buzz of the phone in her pocket and feel like grabbing it and throwing it down the whole length of the corridor. . .

Meep, meep!

Mum locks the car, and we step out of the side street on to Hornsey High Street and head towards the old shop and Nana's flat.

Mum and me are barely talking

171

I'm too mad at her.

And I'm pretty sure she's mad at me.

But I don't care – if she won't listen to me, if she won't even *consider* the fact that Nana might be fine, then there's not much to say, is there?

I've spent the journey mostly staring out of the window, imagining the young version of Nana living here, loving here, all those decades ago. My heart skipped a beat when we drove past a big squat school building and I realized it was her old art college. I nearly pointed it out to Mum, but then didn't bother – she didn't deserve to know. All she can fixate on is this stupid test Nana's got to do on Monday.

So we arrive at the front door to the flat lost in our own little clouds of gloom.

But when Mum throws the door open, we can't help give tandem gasps of surprise. The staircase is no longer a second-hand bookshop. It's bizarrely bare.

"Looks like Dean and Zephyr have been busy while we've been away," says Mum, as a rackety scratching and yelps of welcome break out behind the parrot-painted door up above.

Mr Spinks jumps for joy, his skinny legs boinging

like springs, as soon as we get up there and into the flat. It's as if he's bursting to say, "Well? Well? What do you think?"

I suppose what I think is "Wow. . ."

The hall is huge. Without the cardboard box forest, I see it's practically as big as my bedroom at home.

I'm not sure Angie's so impressed. She's flying around madly above us, wondering where her towering perches have gone. As she swoops and flaps, for a second I think of Pearl alone in her attic cell, her only friend the scrawny, visiting pigeon, till Ruby came along. . .

"Hello?" Mum calls out.

"Hello!" trills Angie, in a perfect imitation of Nana.

"Hi!" Dean booms, from the direction of the living room. "We're in here!"

Me and Mum follow the sound of his voice, staring around like stunned zombies. The room's so large and light now that the hillocks of stuffed bin bags are gone. Lots of the lamps and clutter have been packed away too, downstairs to the shop, or to the outbuilding at the back, I suppose.

Dean and Zephyr are sitting on the sofa, looking

tired and a bit grubby, but perfectly at home. Dean has his feet up on the coffee table, playing around with his laptop. Zephyr's beside him, tanned legs crossed, drinking from a can of Coke.

"You've got so much done!" Mum announces, clearly impressed – and relieved.

"Certainly did!" says Dean. "We were just telling Missy about it. Hey, Missy – your aunt Ren and cousin Scarlet are here. Want to go get Mummy, and then everyone can say hi?"

A sudden panic comes over me as Dean turns the laptop round, and I can see a tanned, blonde little girl on the screen who looks like a mini Zephyr. Behind her, a woman with long blonde hair and a big smile is walking into view.

It's too much. The sherbet in my head is fizzing again.

"Angie's dying to meet you," Dean says to me and Mum.

Even if my brain is fizzing, my face must be doing that shocked/dumb thing it's been so good at today. And of course, Zephyr spots that straightaway.

"Nana named the parrot after my mum?" he says, in that surprised, questioning way he does that winds me up. Like it's ridiculous that I don't know this stuff. He'll probably *love* telling me next that Mr Spinks is named after his sister's hamster or something.

'Cause Zephyr's oh-so-perfect side of the family are *much* more connected to Nana than *my* flaky side, aren't they?

My brain suddenly feels like an overheating computer that's about to crash.

Without saying a word I turn and go, clattering up two flights of stairs with my overnight bag from home banging against the walls and banisters – just like Ruby's awful, drunken uncle in Chapter Three of *The Pearl in the Attic*.

And that's what I want to do right now: be alone – OK, maybe with Mr Spinks because he's just thundered up past me – and lie on the bed, losing myself in the story of Ruby and Pearl so far, so that I don't have to think of the chaos and complication of my *own* life.

With a thwack of wings and a current of air on my face, I realize that Angie is joining me too, but that's all right. Animals and birds are fine; it's only humans I want to close the attic door on right now.

Though I can't even do *that*, since Angie has just

settled herself on the top of the door. She stares down at me as I hurry inside my room and throw my bag on the futon, where Mr Spinks has begun his pre-floop on the bed with a few circling walks. His padding paws are alternately silent on the squashy duvet and rustly as he steps on discarded pages of Chapters One, Two, Three and Four of *The Pearl in the Attic*.

"Dumb dog," I say fondly, quickly leaning down to grab the precious loose pages.

And then I remember my promise to Nana, to say goodnight to the palace for her.

I go over to the window, and examine the drawing pins holding the vintage tea towel/curtain in place. They should be easy to prise off, I think, and then realize the tea towel is bulging a little, as if something behind it is weighing it down.

Flip! And the top left-hand pin pops out. The tea towel slumps.

Flip! The top right-hand pin pops out. Something tumbles down along with the tea towel, and my reflexes kick in, catching the bundle of folded papers in my hand.

So Nana asking me to say goodnight to the palace .. it was the *next* clue, I realize with a smile.

But before I look at Chapter Five – tied with its neat red ribbon – I have something pretty amazing to look at, though at the moment it's only visible through a film of dirt and bird poo. I push at the stiff window, which gives in with a metallic screech, and prop it open with the rusty bar attached to it.

And there it is at last; Alexandra Palace, with its glass domes and arches, its winged stone angel on the apex above the stained glass of the huge Rose Window.

It's spectacular, especially now that the sun is thinking about setting, and the sky is a watercolour wash of moonstone blue and pastel pink. No wonder this place was so special to Nana, and her Manny too. I really need to ask her more about her life as a student here in Hornsey, *and* about the years in Australia. I mean, I remember her once saying that she fell out of love with Grandad Manny but never fell out of love with Britain, and knew she had to come back to it.

Growing up, Nana was just my grandmother, there for me to have fun – *lots* of fun – with.

But now I really want to know everything about her, all her stories and—

"Hi!"

I turn to look at Zephyr in the doorway, all messy hair and goofy smile.

Only he doesn't stay in the doorway; he walks right in.

"When Dad and me were moving stuff, we came across this," he says, holding something out to me.

It's a slightly crumpled photo, of Nana crouched down beside a four-or-five-year-old me in her old garden in Southend. I'm stroking next door's cat, the one that liked to wriggle under the fence and come visit.

"It was behind some bags near the fireplace. I think it must've been on the mantelpiece, but because it wasn't in a frame, I guess it fell down and—"

Zephyr's prattling makes something snap inside me, and sharp-edged words whip right out of my mouth before I can think.

"Get OUT!" I roar at him as I snatch the photo from his hands.

"Huh?" Zephyr says, staring at me like I've gone crazy. "I just thought you'd want this, since it's of Patsy and—"

"Look, she's MY grandmother, and has been for thirteen years," I find myself shouting. "OK?"

A tiny, sensible part of me knows I'm not being fair; knows I'm angry with Mum and the hospital and the strangeness of everything. That I'm angry that the subject of my dad is cropping up again, and I don't know how that makes me feel. And so the furious, mixed-up side of me is really enjoying taking it out on this annoying boy standing in *my* room right now.

"OK! Whatever!" says Zephyr, holding up his hands in surrender as he begins to back away.

"And another thing; I don't need YOU to tell me anything about Nana. I'M looking out for her. 'Cause Nana and me, we have a special connection, and she knows she can trust me and—"

At that moment, in a flutter and a flap of wings, Angie comes between us – and sails straight out of the window and into the night. . .

The Pearl in the Attic

Chapter 5

The tapping was a small sound, but insistent.

At first, still half-sunk in sleep, Ruby supposed it to be raindrops hitting the window. But soon enough, she realized the noise was coming from the ceiling, and hurried out of bed, the seeping light of the dawn helping her find her shawl on the back of the nearby chair quite easily.

As she fastened the shawl about her nightgown, Ruby peered out of the window at the bakery down below, where the door lay wide open, letting the heat and steam of the ovens escape. Uncle Arthur and Wilfred would have been hard at work on the morning bread and rolls for an hour or more already this morning.

As for Aunt Gertrude, she would not rise for some

time yet, till nearer six. By the milky pinks streaking the sky, Ruby supposed it to be a little after five, so she could safely pay Pearl a short visit before the day began proper.

Biting her lip, Ruby turned the handle of the door to her room, carefully inching it open, unsure of the creaks and squeaks it might make.

All was quiet.

Tiptoeing across the chilly oilcloth of the landing, Ruby gently tried the first step of the stairs to the attic. And another, and another. The few creaks there were sounded slight, and surely would not waken Aunt Gertrude, slumbering behind the closed door to her room.

But for a second, Ruby almost lost her nerve, her hand gripping tightly on to the banister, wondering if she should turn back and lock herself away in the safety of her room.

A soft thunk changed her mind.

Up ahead, the attic door had been opened.

"Quick!" mouthed Pearl, waving her on.

With a few nimble steps more, Ruby was in the attic, Pearl closing the door behind them, and they both smiled shyly at each other, hearts racing at the riskiness of their meeting.

As if as pleased to see them as they were to see each other, Pearl's pigeon cooed softly at the little window.

"So you heard me, then?" Pearl asked, two dimples appearing in her cheeks, which Ruby had not noticed when she discovered her hidden here yesterday.

"You shouldn't have knocked – what if Aunt Gertrude had heard?" whispered Ruby, pointing to the side of the attic that was the ceiling to the front bedroom.

"I tapped over there," said Pearl, pointing to the other side of her unmade bed, which she retreated to, curling herself up on the crumpled counterpane and patting the place beside her.

Ruby sat, feeling the crunch of straw stuffing beneath her, like the mattresses back at the cottage.

"So," said Pearl, her eyes sparkling with excitement, "what happened yesterday morning? What was the commotion?"

"Auntie Gertrude didn't tell you?" Ruby replied.

"She didn't come yesterday – it was Mrs Price that saw to me. All she said was that Tante Trudy was very busy."

Ruby knew that to be true; after the morning's

drama, and the tense day that followed, Aunt Gertrude had to work late into the night in the bakery, helping Uncle Arthur make fresh cakes to replace those that were spoiled.

"But from the way Mrs Price held herself, I could tell something *notable* had happened," said Pearl, folding her arms across her chest in the manner of Mrs Price, and pursing her lips the way Ruby had seen the old woman do, as she'd helped clear up the mess.

Despite the memory of yesterday's upset, Ruby's lips curled into a smile at Pearl's talent for mimicry.

"Well, the shop had an order for today, for some rich lady's gathering at her house," Ruby began to tell Pearl, seeing she was keen for *any* news from the outside world, just as a prisoner in solitary confinement would be. "Uncle Arthur had a tray of fondant that was setting, to make decorations for the cakes, and already had a big batch of fondant roses made and laid out to harden."

"And so?" Pearl urged her on. "What was the cause of his shouting? And what of the smashing sound we heard?"

"Nell was the cause ... she had gone through to the bakery to fetch a tray of rolls," Ruby carried on.

"It seems she caught Uncle Arthur's elbow with the edge of the tray. He threw his arm up and sent the whole lot flying. Then he shouted at Nell, and she was so alarmed that she stumbled back and knocked over the fondant that was setting *and* the tray of roses, ruining them all."

"Oh, poor Nell," murmured Pearl, though she had met neither the young woman or her awful uncle in the flesh, Ruby remembered.

"That's not the end of it," Ruby said, drumming her leg and then stopping herself. "Nell ran out into the yard, and Uncle Arthur ran out after her, saying she was dismissed; then he threw a jar of damson jam at her head."

Pearl gasped, putting her hands to her mouth.

"The jar did not hit her, thankfully, but it did go clean through the glass of the back door," Ruby told her quickly, in case Pearl worried for Nell's safety. "Billy saw the whole thing. He told Aunt Gertrude that Uncle Arthur's face was as red as the damson jam!"

The shock seeped from Pearl's face, and a quivering smile took its place. In the second it took for her to slap her hands down on Ruby's, she was shaking with giggles.

The sound of it was so unexpected and delicious. A silly, infectious sound that made Ruby think of her little brothers and sisters at home, playing catch in the cornfields.

Before Ruby knew it, some dam of sadness and dread burst inside her, and she found herself giggling too, rocking on the bed, gasping for breath, her hands clutching Pearl's...

Until she realized she was the only one laughing.

Lifting her head, she saw Pearl's eyes wide and staring at something behind her.

Or someone.

As Ruby's turned her head to see who was there, she felt the warmth of laughter turn to the chill prickle of alarm.

Aunt Gertrude stood in the attic doorway, fixing her blank gaze upon both girls.

For a long moment they all seemed frozen, Ruby holding her breath, waiting for the bite of the furious words that must come.

But they did not. Aunt Gertrude suddenly stirred from her shocked stillness. She hurried into the attic, shut the door behind her and crumpled to the floor in cloud of puffed cotton nightgown. Her hands covered her face as she sobbed.

"Tante! It's all right, Ruby is my friend," Pearl burst out, leaping off the makeshift bed and rushing to the older woman's side. "She won't tell. Will you, Ruby?"

Pearl glanced back at Ruby, her expression as well as her words urging her new friend to help her reassure their aunt.

"No, no, of course not," Ruby said quickly, picking the skin of her nails. She didn't know Aunt Gertrude in the way Pearl did. It was not her place to offer her comfort. But to see a grown woman in such distress was disturbing, and Ruby wished there was something more she could say or do. . .

"So, please, darling Tante Trudy," said Pearl, slipping a skinny arm around her aunt's shoulders, "*please* don't worry."

At those words, Aunt Gertrude raised her head. She looked beaten and broken.

"But all I can *do* is worry, Pearl!" she said with a choke in her throat. "I brought you here, but what now? How can I make you safe? Truly, I am at my wits' end. . ."

Aunt Gertrude was desperate, her mind fogged with fear. Fear of her husband and what he was capable of, Ruby realized. What would become of

Pearl at his hands; how he might punish his wife for her deception?

But suddenly, Ruby stirred as an idea came to her. With Father, to offer a thought or suggestion risked a slap for her cheek. But Father wasn't here.

She looked at the woman and the girl by the door, clinging to each other as if they'd found themselves on a sinking ship.

What Ruby had found was her voice, and it rang out clear and strong.

"I think I know what to do. . ."

She was to be known as Polly.

It was the name of Ruby's youngest sister and would come readily to mind whenever Ruby had to address the new shop girl.

Aunt Gertrude had barely spoken when Ruby first suggested the plan, but her face – a picture of hope and possibility and relief – said it all. After that, she and Ruby had set to work very quickly, lifting the tin bath up to the attic together, each gripping a metal handle. They had boiled kettles and took them in turn to Pearl, so that she could bathe and wash her waist-length sheaf of hair.

And when the shop opened at seven a.m., "Polly"

looked just grand, in Nell's old apron and with her red hair dark and still damp, but scraped back into a neat, tight bun.

"Thank you! Come again!" Pearl called out after the customer taking her leave.

Aunt Gertrude, holding the door open, shot a proud look at her orphaned niece.

All morning, Pearl had worked hard and she had worked well.

Before her father was taken ill, he had been a clerk in a hardware shop in Hastings, Pearl had told Ruby, in the snatches of time between the comings and goings of customers. She had helped out sometimes, becoming quick with coins and change, and earning a ha'penny here and there for her trouble.

The bell above the shop door tinkled as Aunt Gertrude closed it, and she went back to the business of dressing the window with Vienna breads and fancies.

"Try again!" Pearl urged Ruby, now that the shop was quiet. She reached under the counter for a paper bag, and placed it on the glass countertop.

Ruby gave her a little smile, picked up the pencil by the till, and wondered what to write this time.

And then it came to her...

Ruby and Pearl.

"Ha! 'Ruby and Pearl' – the Gem Girls!" Pearl whispered to her, linking an arm in hers. "And how well you have done your letters!"

It was true, Ruby's handwriting was improving already, with Pearl's encouragement and with just a few minutes' practice here and there over the last few hours. As her friend had promised, a pencil was so much easier to use than the scratchy ink pens of her old and hated schoolroom. And to see her words form neatly, thanks to the spectacles, was quite wonderful. For the very first time, Ruby could see the pleasure that might be had, writing thoughts down on a page and—

A hand reached across the glass and snatched the bag away from her, before hastily crushing it into a ball.

Ruby glanced up, wondering what she had done to displease her aunt – then understood as soon as she heard the heavy footfall and grunted breaths coming from the storeroom.

"Sir, I beg your pardon, but it is Saturday and I am due my wages!" Billy's voice drifted through behind the bulk of Uncle Arthur. "And you did not pay me for last week, Mr Wells..."

Aunt Gertrude shot a look at both girls; it was time.

Time for Uncle Arthur to meet "Polly".

For this was the scheme Ruby had suggested: Pearl, in the guise of Polly, might work in the shop awhile – though still smuggled up in the attic at night – till such time as Aunt Gertrude could provide "Polly" with a letter of good conduct. That one vital piece of correspondence would allow Pearl to try for a position as a live-in maid in some pleasant house nearby. Which would mean on Sundays, when the shop was closed and a maid would have a half-day, Aunt Gertrude and Pearl and Ruby could meet, stroll through the hilly gardens of Alexandra Palace, sit in the tearooms there and talk of happy things together. What a joy that would be!

But it would only be a joy if the Pearl was not found out.

Ruby and Pearl gave the merest of nods to Aunt Gertrude, and quickly went to busy themselves about the shop.

"Wages? Wages, you say? Who are you to tell me when you'll get your wages, Billy Blake?" roared Uncle Arthur, appearing in the back doorway with a laden wooden tray. "You'll get them when

I'm good and ready to give 'em to you, and not a moment before. . . Now will someone clear this mess? HURRY!"

Ruby quickly scurried over to the table Uncle Arthur wanted to set his tray down upon. There were some boxes and string and a pair of scissors laid there from cakes Aunt Gertrude had recently parceled up for a customer. All Ruby needed to do was sweep them to the side and there'd be plenty of room for—

The crushing pain took Ruby's breath away.

She glanced into her uncle's eyes and saw no apology for dropping the heavy tray on to her fingers. It was, in fact, the opposite: a gloating look like that of a bully at school who might trip you up or tip your inkwell over your work and then dare you to tell on them.

Lowering her eyes, saying nothing, Ruby withdrew, biting her lip to stop herself from crying as she hugged her throbbing fingers in her other hand.

"Are you STILL here, Billy Blake?" she heard her uncle say, now that he was done with her.

Through the haze of blinked-back tears, Ruby risked a glance in the direction of the delivery boy. He was hovering – cap in hand – just inside the storeroom. His eyes darted at her, seeing all, and yet he bravely persisted with his cause.

192

"But, sir," said Billy, "it has been some time now and my mother is behind with the rent and—"

Uncle Arthur fixed the lad with a silencing stare, as if he were a bull about to charge – or a baker about to use his fists.

Ruby peeked across at Pearl, and saw that her face was quite ashen. Of course, she had never met this man in the flesh. She had only heard of him as Aunt Gertrude's bullying second husband. To her, he must appear like a monster in a fairy tale. Standing behind the counter opposite her, Ruby could do nothing but hope Pearl would not faint. The only way her plan would work was if Uncle Arthur saw "Polly" as a hard-working and acceptable replacement for the dismissed Nell.

And likewise, Uncle Arthur had never set eyes on Pearl, and must never hear her true name spoken – so no wonder Aunt Gertrude had hidden away the evidence of Ruby's most recent writing.

For now, it was as if all in the shop stood still, like some tableau, breaths held, pain suppressed, waiting for some violence of word or blow to follow, or for a faint that might undo the only scheme that was supposed to save Pearl from the poorhouse. . .

But the cheerful tinkle of the shop-door bell

broke the uncomfortable spell.

The presence of a customer worked like magic; Uncle Arthur did not strike Billy, Pearl did not faint.

"Come tomorrow afternoon, after I have done the accounting," Uncle Arthur gruffly told Billy. "I'll have your wages for you then."

Ruby took a deep breath, and went to take the cakes from the tray and fill the shelves – but hesitated when she saw who the customer was. The girl with the knickerbockers, from Colonel Samuel Cody's Wild West show.

The girl smiled directly at Ruby, but her eyes seemed questioning. Had she been looking in the window before she came in? Perhaps she had witnessed the deliberate injury Uncle Arthur had inflicted. . .

"Can I help you?" asked Pearl, since she was closest to the curiously dressed girl. Her voice was more childlike and uncertain than it had been when she had served other customers. But, Ruby supposed, when Pearl had served those ladies and gentlemen, Uncle Arthur had not been looming close by.

"I was just wondering if you might put a poster in the window, for the show happening up at Alexandra Pal—"

"No! D'you presume my fine window is a billboard, missy?" Uncle Arthur bellowed at the girl, looking her up and down with a scowl of disgust at her apparel.

"Of course, sir, I understand," the girl said with an easy smile, and turned instead to browse the tempting cakes in the displays.

A cold shiver ran the length of Ruby's spine as she saw Uncle Arthur now glower at the stranger behind his shop counter.

"And who is this?" he demanded of Aunt Gertrude, his eyes boring into Pearl.

"This is Polly. She came in this morning asking for work, and I gave her a trial for the day," Aunt Gertrude answered him, with remarkable calm under the circumstances, Ruby noticed admiringly.

"You let some little chit come in off the street without consulting me?" Uncle Arthur replied, his look and voice a shade dangerous, rage brewing just below the surface, customer or no customer.

"With Nell gone, we were short-handed in the rush this morning," said Aunt Gertrude, matter-of-factly. "Customers were arriving and leaving again straightaway, when they saw the queue. When Polly came in, she seemed presentable and had done shop work before. I am not paying her for today, Arthur; she has done quite well so far, but she knows that if it is not up to scratch then she will not return tomorrow."

A frown came on to Uncle Arthur's broad, sweaty forehead as he considered what his wife had just said.

"Well, we don't want to be losing customers' money," he grumbled, swayed by the issue of plain profit. "She may stay till the end of the day, and then we'll see. . ."

Uncle Arthur turned away, barging past Billy.

"Might you come to the show, even if it is not possible to put up the poster?" the cheerful girl asked Aunt Gertrude as soon as Uncle Arthur had lumbered off, with Billy trailing after him.

She unrolled the advertising bill to show Aunt Gertrude. Pearl hurried around the counter to stand by Ruby.

"Oh, my!" she cried in delight at the vision of the colonel on his rearing horse.

"I'm sorry, but I don't think so," said Aunt Gertrude, though her words sounded hesitant as she saw the look on Pearl's face. "My husband . . . he would not like it. And anyway, we have no money to spare for this type of entertainment."

The girl smiled broadly and tilted her head to one side.

"Well, I have no money to spare for cakes such as these beauties," she said. "So may I propose something?"

A little flicker of excitement lit up inside Ruby, making her momentarily forget her pained fingers. She exchanged a quick look with Pearl, whose eyes were saucer-wide with wonder as she too waited to hear what the girl had to say.

"Um ... very well," said Aunt Gertrude, a little flustered. "Say your piece."

"If you were to give me a few of your fine cakes," the girl began with a wry grin, "I could let you come and watch my act without paying?"

"Oh, I don't know. As I say, my husband—"

"Oh, I quite understand that a man of your husband's ... temperament may not be amused by the show. But I'm sure these two young ladies would love it!" the girl said confidently, interrupting Auntie Gertrude's protestations. "My aeronautic act is quite spectacular! I ascend into the sky by means of hot air balloon, and descend by parachute! Dolly Shepherd, by the way. Pleased to meet you."

Now looking at her properly, Ruby realized with

some surprise that this girl, this performer, was barely older than she and Pearl.

"I ... I ... am Mrs Brandt. Mrs Wells, I mean," stumbled Aunt Gertrude, thrown to find the girl holding a hand out to shake hers. "Pleased to make your acquaintance. Er, Ruby ... would you like to make up a small box for Miss Shepherd?"

Pearl gave such a squeal of delight, her dimples deep with the thrill of what this girl – this Miss Shepherd – had suggested and what their aunt had agreed to.

"So I shall see you ladies later today?" asked the girl, as she pointed to a Madeira tart, a langue de chat cream horn, an iced cake with jellied strawberries on top and a dainty basket-shaped confection of sponge, jam and fondant flowers. Ruby worked quickly, neatly placing Dolly's selection in a ready-made box. She'd use ribbon to tie it, and fasten it neatly with the biggest bow, no matter how much her fingers were stinging.

"Not today; tomorrow, Sunday. The girls will come when the shop is shut," said Aunt Gertrude, attempting to sound as if she were in control and had not been railroaded into something unexpected.

"Perfect!" said Dolly, taking the proffered box

from Ruby. "It is the last day of the performance before the show moves to France... Be there at two!"

With a smile and a wave, Dolly took her leave, the bell tinkling in her wake.

As soon as she was gone, Pearl ran to wrap her arms around a startled Aunt Gertrude.

Watching, smiling, Ruby licked a little smudge of cream from the tip of one of her bruised fingers.

The sweetness burst on her tongue.

Just as Pearl had – in such a short time – brought such a dash of sweetness to Ruby's world...

The Lost and the Found

I'm making a total mess of this.

The Sellotape won't stick to the metal of the street light base, and I *have* to get these posters up. Angie's been missing all night, and the longer she's gone. . .

Oh, this is a nightmare. If I hadn't opened that stupid window, I could be lying in my bed now, rereading the most tense chapter yet of Nana's novel, and daydreaming about where the next one's hidden.

Instead, I'm wrapping half a roll of tape around a piece of A4 paper that's starting to rip, and trying not to cry in public.

"Hello, Mr Spinks!"

My fingers are so tangled in the misbehaving

tape that it takes me a second to turn and see who's talking to Nana's dog.

It's a smiley lady in a red polka-dot apron, tidying away a coffee cup from a table outside a café.

I spotted this café yesterday morning, on my first walk out with Mr Spinks. Close up, the hanging baskets of flowers are beautiful, and so are the amazing bejewelled hanging lamps I've just spotted hanging inside.

It's strange how wrong first impressions can be. On Thursday night, when me and Mum first arrived here, I thought the high street was a bit forgotten and grim. Pockets of it might still seem that way, but if you look – I mean, *really* look – at a place you can see so much. This morning I came across an ancient church tower and graveyard at the far end of the street, an original stone horse and cattle drinking trough, beautifully ornate old pubs, cafés that range from Caribbean to Italian to Thai to Turkish. There might be nasty plastic signage above lots of shops, but I've spotted snatches of stained glass and gorgeous original tiles with art nouveau flower patterns in all sorts of delicious colours.

But what I *haven't* spotted anywhere is a grey parrot.

And that's why I ran off a bunch of posters on Nana's printer this morning, and have walked up and down the high street sticking them up wherever I can, while Mum, Dean and Zephyr carry on with emptying the flat of its clutter.

"You're looking after Patsy's dog?" says the lady, who's now crouched down and scratching Mr Spinks's ears.

"Um, yes ... I'm her granddaughter," I say shyly. "Me and my mum are staying at her flat. So you know her?"

"Oh, yes! Patsy's one of our best customers. She likes to sit out here with Mr Spinks and watch the world go by," says the dark-haired lady, straightening up. "And you know *I* found her on Thursday evening, when she had her fall; we'd just finished tidying up here and were on our way home. How is she?"

"Oh! Uh, thank you so much for helping her!" I stumble at the surprise of meeting Nana's rescuer. "And she's doing OK. I mean, she's broken quite a few bones, but she's still pretty cheerful."

"Of course, she is! Wonderful Patsy," says the woman, beaming. "Will you tell her everyone at the café sends their love?"

I don't mean to.

I can't help it.

But after searching the streets last night, losing my voice from calling Angie's name, spending the night lying in bed watching the open window in the sloped ceiling and hoping against hope that she'd fly back in, I am in pieces.

And how will I tell Nana, my wonderful nana, when we go in to visit her later...?

As I cry great, wracking, nose-dripping sobs, I find myself in a hug, with my back being patted and some soothing words being said in a different language. When I finally catch my breath and look up, two girls from the café are there, one offering me a bundle of serviettes to dry my eyes and wipe away the snot, while the other comforts Mr Spinks, who's staring up at me and rocking nervously from paw to paw.

"She'll be fine, your grandmother. She's a strong, independent lady!" says the café owner.

"It's not just that," I say, hiccuping. "Her parrot escaped last night. I have to find it..."

"Oh, no – not Angie!" says the café owner, as she and the girls take a look at the poster and pull sad, worried faces.

The poster says *Missing*, of course, with a photo on it of Angie that Nana had sent to Dean. My number and Mum's is underneath, and Dean said he'll pay a reward if anyone finds her.

"Maybe she's flown to Ally Pally Park," suggests one of the girls. "What bird could resist the sight of all those trees?"

Hope and worry merge in a knot in my tummy. The girl could be right, but if Angie's in the park, she could be in trouble again, same as she was when Nana found her. An exotic outsider, being mobbed by the locals.

"What's the quickest way to the park?" I ask.

The café owner and the girls quickly explain. But as soon as I'm on the side road they pointed at, I don't need to remember a word they said – Mr Spinks confidently leads the way, waddling perkily on the route of one of his well-worn walks.

And just a few minutes later, I'm there, on a huge meadow of grass, where joggers are jogging, kids are kicking footballs, dogs are rough and tumbling.

Directly ahead of me, a wooded hillside gently rises up to the palace itself.

The grand yellow brick building that's so tangled up in Nana's history, the history of Nana's flat and shop, the history of the real or not-so-real Ruby and Pearl. . .

Suddenly I feel too small out here in this vast expanse, and flop down on the nearest bench, dropping my head into my hands, while Mr Spinks tries to help by resting his head on my knees and licking my elbow.

But how can I hope to find Angie here? Where would I even start? I can hardly croak her name, since I yelled my throat raw last night, and probably drove everyone in the surrounding flats mad.

I wish I was like Ruby, in that last chapter of Nana's story, when she came up with the idea of getting Pearl working in the shop, hiding in plain sight.

I wish, like her, I knew in this moment what to do. . .

"Arf!" Mr Spinks gives a small yelp.

And then I hear a shout.

"Arf!" Mr Spinks yelps again, and I feel the weight of his chin lift from my knees.

The shout comes again.

I glance up, and see the tousled blonde hair, the board shorts and tanned legs. Zephyr is spinning around, eyes to the skies, hands to his mouth, calling Angie's name.

"ARF!" Mr Spinks yelps louder, and pulls himself away so fast, so unexpectedly, that his lead slips right out of my hand.

Great, I've managed to lose *both* of Nana's pets in quick succession. . .

"Mr Spinks! Come back!" I squeak, rising up from the bench.

But he's safe enough.

Zephyr's face bursts into a smile as he sees the dog hurtling towards him, and scoops the fat pooch into his arms.

I flump back on to the bench, feeling useless and sad and empty.

Zephyr, meanwhile, is laughing his head off, as Mr Spinks frantically licks his face clean.

"No luck?" asks my cousin as he plonks the dog on the bench next to me and sits down.

"No luck," I say, and realize I've been crying again.

We sit in silence for a bit, a girl, a dog and a boy on a bench.

"I'm sorry if . . . if me and Dad being here has made everything more complicated or difficult for you or whatever," Zephyr says finally.

OK, so I was already feeling useless and sad and empty, but now I can add *bad* to that.

"It's not really your fault," I say with a shrug, knowing that's true now that crying's washed some of my rage away. "I mean, our families kind of overlap, which makes it more obvious that *my* version is a bit rubbish compared to yours."

"How's ours better?" asks Zephyr, sounding genuinely confused.

"Well, there's just me and Mum. There hasn't even been Nana for a while, since the two of them bicker and fight and fell out properly last year," I say. "And then *your* side sounds all happy and busy and close, with two parents and a sister and grandparents and everything, AND you seem to be closer to Nana than us!"

It feels all right to say that stuff. Like saying it makes the fog in my head clear a little.

"Yeah, getting to know Patsy's been fun the last few months, but it was for a sad reason, don't forget, with Grandad dying," says Zephyr. "And lots of things haven't been great or easy for us. Dad's company didn't make any money for a long time, and we were pretty broke, and that caused arguments between Mum and Dad. Then there's the fact that my mum and my gran – that's Grandad Manny's second wife – they can rub each other up the wrong way. As for Great-Aunt Sita; she's not been well and Mum's round there a lot looking after her—"

"Wait," I say, "Sita lives *near* you?"

"Yeah, she emigrated to Australia years ago," Zephyr replies. "She's just a couple of streets away. And then there's Missy; she's SUCH a whiner. Man, can my sister moan! 'Zeph got three more fries than I did!'"

I give a little laugh, in spite of myself.

"And don't even get me *started* on our names," Zephyr carries on, getting all animated now. "My mum's a bit of a hippy, and she called us Zephyr and Mistral, after winds. I mean, *winds*. Can you imagine the teasing I get in class when kids find out? Making farting noises all over the place?"

I'm laughing again. He's pretty funny. Who knew?

"Well, I suppose it's no different to naming people after *stones*," I suggest. "Like … like Ruby or Pearl. And hey, don't forget, I'm named after a colour!"

"Of course, yeah." Zephyr nods and smiles. "So who came up with that? Your mum, or your dad?"

He shoots me a sideways look. He's fishing for

info, and up till now, he'd have been the last person I'd've chosen to tell. But, hey . . . why not? He is sort of family, I suppose.

"My mum chose the name. My dad. . ." I hesitate. "Well, he doesn't know my name. He doesn't even know I exist."

"Wow, sounds complicated," says Zephyr.

"It is a bit," I agree, then take a big breath. "My mum and him met through a dating site. They went out together for a few months, and really liked each other. But then my dad got his, like, *dream* job, working for some charity in Ecuador."

"South America?" Zephyr checks his geography facts.

"Uh-huh," I say with a nod. "Mum and him broke up on good terms, because, you know, they decided it's hard to meet up and go to the movies when you live on different continents. . ."

Zephyr laughs, which makes me relax a bit. I never get the chance to talk about this stuff to anyone. I once tried with Bella and Aisha, but they ended up staring at me with something like pity crossed with embarrassment, so I changed the subject pretty quick and never went back there.

"Things got complicated after my dad moved

away," I carry on, "'cause Mum found out she was expecting *me*."

"Wow, again!" Zephyr mutters.

"Anyway, Mum decided not to tell him. She thought it wasn't fair; they'd split up, he'd gone to another country; she wasn't going to mess with his new life. And so it's just us!"

"That was brave, or something," Zephyr says, sounding uncertain. "How do *you* feel about it?"

OK, so it's my turn to wow. No one's ever asked me that before.

"It's all right," I say, but I'm not totally sure it is. "Nana always says, '*Never regret the past, but always look to the future*'. She brought Mum up to think like that, and I suppose I do too."

But do I?

And Nana ... that might be her life's motto, but she's doing an *awful* lot of looking at the past at the moment.

Nana – now she's back in my mind again, and so is the guilt. I can't help but let out a long, low groan.

"What?" says Zephyr, as he and Mr Spinks stare at me.

"What about Angie!" I burst out. "How do I tell Nana she's missing?"

"Well, you don't," Zephyr says matter-of-factly. "Let's not worry her for now, and we'll hopefully get Angie back before Patsy's allowed out of hospital. And look – I did a search online and found these brilliant photos of the shop from years and years ago. I'll show them to her later. We can make it all about that."

"Thank you," I say, taken aback at Zephyr's thoughtfulness.

He's holding his phone up between us, about level with Mr Spinks's nose, and I squint to see better.

To see first an old black-and-white photo, with fancy lettering above it that reads *Brandt's Baker and Confectioners*. A boy with a delivery bike stands outside, grinning at the camera.

My heart starts thundering. Is it Billy, the delivery lad? For real, I mean? Or did Nana already do research and find this photo, which helped her to make up her story?

"That one looks seriously old, but check out *this* one," says Zephyr, flicking to an image that seems like it must be from the 1940s, by the looks of the rolled hairstyles the women are wearing.

There's a muddle of smiling people in this: a young couple, an older couple, three young boys, with quite an old lady leaning on the arm of the tallest of them. The shop has a newer sign; it's now called *Brandt & Blake*.

So the shop below Nana's flat really *was* a bakery, and for a pretty long time. And it really *was* called Brandt's.

More inspiration? Or more pieces of a true story?

"Pretty cool, eh?" As he talks, I watch the easy, charming smile on Zephyr's face, and realize two things.

I'm totally rubbish at first impressions, and that doesn't only mean random North London streets. It means cousins too.

And maybe I need to share more than just a parrot search and an unknown dad story with Zephyr.

Maybe I should share the *The Pearl in the Attic* with him too. . .

I'm so lost in thoughts about my possibly fantastic new-found cousin that I jump when Zephyr's phone jangles with a text message.

"Hey – it's from Patsy." He reads from the screen. "She says she can't wait to see us today. Then she says can I give you her number. Oh, and she wants to tell you, if number five is done, then look out for six beginning to rise. . . What does *that* mean?"

"It means I need your help," I say to Zephyr. "How are you at solving riddles?"

"Bring it on!" says Zephyr, raising his eyebrows at me. "Just as long as you don't, y'know, *shout* at me again. . ."

"Promise," I say, feeling embarrassed at the way I acted last night.

I hold my pinkie up to him and we shake on it, with a lick of our fingers from Mr Spinks to seal the deal. . .

"Any sign of Angie?" says Uncle Dean as we come across him with the laundry basket full of yellow plastic ducks at his feet.

He's unlocking the side gate, presumably to take them through the passage to the outbuilding in the yard: the old bakery. I haven't made it out there yet – but I'm about to.

"Nope. We walked around the park for half an hour," I tell Uncle Dean. "We tried whistling and calling for her –"

"– and barking," Dean adds, nodding down at Mr Spinks.

"– but all we saw were pigeons and crows."

"Well, hopefully, when Angie gets hungry

enough, she'll find her way home," Uncle Dean suggests, giving me a comforting squeeze of the arm. "Or maybe when she fancies a cup of tea, eh?"

I smile, hoping he's right.

"Anyway, will we take these in for you, Dad, if you want to go and get more stuff?" Zephyr suggests.

"Great," says Dean. "Do you want to open up, Scarlet, and Zephyr can deal with the wildlife?"

With that, Uncle Dean heads back towards the flat's front door, and I rattle our way into the alleyway with the clunky keys, while Zephyr grabs up the collection of ducks.

"Maybe we should make an arrow out of these on the roof, to guide Angie back," Zephyr jokily suggests, as I lead the way with Mr Spinks.

The door to the bakery is open; I guess Uncle Dean and Mum have been busy while we've been away.

I gaze inside; an ugly strip light illuminates the whole space, which is stacked high with the boxes, books and bin bags that Uncle Dean and Zephyr moved out of the hall, stairways and living room yesterday while we were away in Chelmsford.

But what's *not* ugly are the old but still glossy white tiles that cover all the walls, just like they were described in Chapter Two of *The Pearl in the*

Attic. And I'm hoping to see the old bread oven too – where bread rises ... that was Zephyr's guess to solve Nana's clue.

"Oh ... it's not the original one," I say, spotting some modern contraption of metal and black plastic knobs and handles. I guess if this was still a bakery for years after Ruby and Pearl's time, then certain things would've had to be modernized.

"Yeah, but it still made bread," says Zephyr, putting the basket of ducks down.

He gives Mr Spinks one to chew before he sets off clambering around and over the general clutter. I watch him peer through dusty glass doors – and then hear him whoop as he hauls one open.

"Is this what we're looking for?" he asks, holding up the ribbon-wrapped folded papers.

"Don't you dare!" I say, when I see Zephyr about to undo the bow. "Come on up to the attic – you've got a bit of catching up to do before we read *that* chapter..."

"Good to see you two are having fun!" I hear Mum's voice say.

She's just coming through the bakery doorway holding metal poles – a dismantled clothes rack from the second floor, I think.

"Anyway, Dean says you haven't found Angie," Mum says to me. "And I just wanted to say, don't beat yourself up, Scarlet. I mean, hopefully she'll come back, but Nana might have to accept that long term, she might not be able to care for her pets if—"

"I don't want to hear this, Mum," I say, moving to get past her.

"I know you don't, darling," Mum replies. "Which is why I downloaded you this. . ."

Mum hands me a document that's headed, *Explaining Dementia to Children and Young People.*

"No, thanks," I say snippily. "I've got something better to read: Nana's *amazing* story."

So Mum is still determined to think Nana's losing her mind.

When really, it's Mum who's losing hers, if she believes that. . .

The Pearl in the Attic

Chapter 6

The girls were agog.

The delights of the park were so very, very many. There were signs to an outdoor swimming lido, a racetrack along the flat at the foot of the hill, a boating lake, and a little rollicking railway ride that was called a rollercoaster.

"What a place this is!" Pearl said joyfully, her arm hooked in Ruby's. "When I'm employed as a maid, I'll save all my money and we'll come here *every* week!"

Ruby squeezed Pearl's arm, touched by her friend's kind offer. She doubted that a kitchen maid's wages would run to much, but it would be more than Ruby would ever earn at Uncle Arthur's, where she had bed and board and should be grateful of it.

As they walked and talked and daydreamed uphill through the grounds towards the palace itself, Ruby and Pearl stared about them at families strolling, children laughing and gambolling. Rich men in their black hats and fine suits escorted rich ladies in dresses abounding in tucks and pleats and flounces. Not-so-rich folk were in their pressed Sunday best, with clean collars and polished boots. Girls wearing jaunty hats adorned with bunches of violets or clusters of cherries smiled sweetly into the faces of their beaus.

Ruby and Pearl had no finery of their own, but felt grand enough this Sunday afternoon. They'd brushed each other's hair till it shone, and decided they would wear it down, in thick braids tied with ribbon Pearl kept in a small bag of sewing stuff and scraps brought from her home. Over their similar skirts of grey and brown and their plain, high-necked white blouses, they both had about their shoulders pretty shawls lent to them by Aunt Gertrude, shawls she had worn in former, gladder times, it seemed to Ruby.

When Uncle Arthur had left for the Three Compasses pub along the road, Aunt Gertrude had taken both the shawls up to the attic, where the girls had been quietly talking together, Ruby mending holes in her black stockings while Pearl stitched a little piece of tapestry.

As she presented the shawls to the delighted girls – a lacy, scallop-edged blue wool one for Ruby, a delicate black shawl with embroidered red roses for Pearl – Ruby noticed they had been folded for some time and smelled of lavender to keep off the moths, as if they had been kept in a drawer or cupboard for many months, if not years.

Aunt Gertrude had put away her good things along with her good memories when she married Uncle Arthur, Ruby suspected. She would not even come along with them this afternoon, as if she were undeserving of happiness.

"Shush, no," she'd said at their final entreaty earlier, as she looked anxiously down the road towards the pub, waving them off. "Go and enjoy yourselves. He'll be snoring on the settee by the time you're back, but take care all the same!"

They'd felt wretched for Aunt Gertrude as they hurried away, but giddiness at what was to come had them both forget their aunt, the shop and their dreaded uncle very quickly.

"Look! They strut like the bird that comes to your window!" Ruby whispered now as some young ladies glided by them who must have been wearing the latest S-shaped corset that made their chests stick out and gave them the gait of a preening pigeon.

"Coo! Coo!" Pearl muttered, a touch too loudly, and both girls broke into giggles when the one of the young ladies turned to scowl at them over her shoulder.

"Come on!" Ruby said gaily, breaking into a run and pulling Pearl up a different path in the flower-bed-lined hillside. "It must be near two o'clock now. . ."

Great wide steps came in view that let up to a terrace around the palace, and billboards abounded, advertising the Wild West show that would take place inside.

But Ruby and Pearl, with nothing in their pockets for the entry price, were here only for Dolly's show – and they could now see crowds on a clearing to the right of the palace, and hear a tremendous hissing noise too.

"Where do you suppose the balloon is?" asked Pearl as they hurried closer to the crowds.

"Look, there!" Ruby said, pointing as a large dome

made of some kind of light-coloured cloth began to bob and billow above the heads of those watching.

Quickly, the girls hurried across and begged people's pardon as they gently wriggled and squeezed their way through.

And then they could go no further; a fence of rope had been constructed to provide a wide circle in the grass for the *Astounding Aeronautic Display, starring Miss Dolly Shepherd!*, as a large poster nearby proclaimed.

Within the circle a few men milled. Two were tending a fire, throwing straw into a small stone-ringed pit, and watching as the smoke gathered with hisses and whooshes inside the ever-expanding, ever-rising balloon. Another pair were checking the tightness of ropes that tethered the balloon to a heavy-looking carriage, weighed down further with sandbags.

One more man, dressed in his Wild Western–style garb and hat of a cowboy, watched the proceedings with a smile on his face and hands on his hips.

And then there was Dolly.

As she strutted in her suit of knickerbockers and long-fitted jacket, with laced-up boots that nearly reached her knees, she looked quite marvellous, Ruby thought, her chest heaving with admiration.

Dolly's arms were held aloft as she casually went about pinning a loose curl in her lusciously piled hair.

At least, she was attempting to pin the curl, but perhaps the lack of mirror was proving tricky. As soon as she saw Ruby and Pearl, her eyes lit up, and she beckoned them to come under the rope and join her.

"Everyone is watching us!" Pearl whispered to Ruby as they shyly went to join the older girl.

"I know," Ruby whispered back, thinking her cheeks must be the colour of the roses on her friend's shawl.

"You came!" Dolly said cheerfully. "Now could one of you pin me tight? I don't want to land at the end with my hair untangling about me as if I had tumbled off a haystack."

Ruby, who had so loved to braid the hair of her mother and little sisters, stepped over to help at once, glad to take a handful of pins from Dolly and have a job to do as the mutterings of "Who *are* they?" buzzed from the crowd. She began to fix and pin, only wincing a little at the small stabs of pain she still felt in two of her battered fingers.

"Are you frightened?" Pearl asked Dolly, her eyes wide with excitement.

"Not a bit! It's the most wonderful feeling. To be so high above everyone and everything, to see the birds spin around and spy on me, wondering what I am doing in their world . . . it's quite, quite magical," said Dolly, with a faraway look in her eyes. "And it's certainly better than being a waitress!"

"You were a waitress before this?" Pearl repeated.

Ruby was as startled as her friend. She could barely imagine a performer like Dolly doing such a mundane job, but said nothing, due to the pins she had placed in her mouth.

"Yes – in the tearooms," said Dolly, pointing at the palace. "I worked there till last Saturday."

"What?" Pearl exclaimed. "How? I mean. . ."

Dolly's shoulders heaved as she laughed.

"I can hardly believe it myself!" she said. "But it's true; when my shift finished in the tearoom, I came by here, where Colonel Cody was setting up this attraction. Another girl was practising the trick, but she did not want to go through with it. Then the colonel saw me watching, and asked if I was an adventurous sort. Luckily for him, I am. And so with a bit of training, I found myself in the air in no time!"

Standing behind Dolly's shoulder, Ruby saw the

expression of amazement and longing on Pearl's face. Perhaps being shut up in the attic with only the clouds and birds for company these last weeks made her yearn for the freedom Dolly had.

"And now, after this, you go to France?" she asked breathlessly of the aeronaut.

"France, and then we tour the whole of Europe," Dolly announced. "And Colonel Cody hopes to take us on to Australia after that."

Pearl's blue eyes widened, as if someone had told her of the greatest secret.

"Australia? Really?" she gasped.

But Ruby was now gasping for her own reasons. She could see Colonel Cody himself striding over to them, touching his tan leather hat in greeting.

"Pleasure to meet you, ladies," said the colonel in a rich, rolling American drawl, addressing Ruby and Pearl as if they were more than just young, gawky shop girls. "Any friend of Dolly's is surely a friend of mine."

Ruby, her pinning now done, shyly came around and shook the hand that was being offered. Pearl did the same, her dimples twinkling in her cheeks.

"Now, I'm thinkin'," the colonel continued, scratching his splendid beard and shooting a mischievous look at Dolly, "might you ladies be interested in making this last performance of the week one the folks here'll be talkin' about for years?"

Dolly was laughing, already sure of what he was asking, even if Ruby and Pearl had no clue.

"Yes!" Pearl burst out, without knowing what task he was suggesting.

"Ah, now both of you are very lovely ladies, but perhaps you, my dear," Colonel Cody said directly to Pearl, "are just a little lighter. Will you come over this way with Dolly and me... ?"

Before Ruby knew it, she was handed the shawl that had been plucked from around Pearl's shoulders, and was being ushered to wait near the carriage by one of the men with their shirtsleeves rolled up.

"What's happening?" she asked him as she saw Colonel Cody talking earnestly to Pearl. Dolly must have felt Ruby's concerned stare, and gave her a carefree wink.

"See the trapeze?" said the man, pointing at the balloon, which hovered now at around the height of two men from the ground.

From the bottom of it hung a sort of swing, consisting of ropes tied to a bar.

"Yes," muttered Ruby, unnerved now as she saw another fellow fit a type of bag on to Dolly's shoulders, while Colonel Cody continued to talk to a nodding Pearl.

"Well, Dolly holds on to the trapeze, is lifted into the air by it, then—"

"LADIES and GENTLEMEN, BOYS and GIRLS!" Colonel Cody now turned and boomed to the waiting crowd. "All this week the lovely MISS DOLLY SHEPHERD has been ASTONISHING audiences daily with her daring flights... With NO thought to her own safety, she has..."

As the colonel boomed on with many choice words about the spectacle they were about to see, Ruby's ears grew deaf. All she could see was that Pearl was being strapped to Dolly by means of a tight harness, as Dolly talked insistently to her and Pearl listened just as earnestly.

"...you will witness a feat SO rare," Colonel Cody boomed on, "as not ONE but TWO young ladies take this risky journey into the skies..."

And then the two girls smiled – and before Ruby could think to rescue her friend, the trapeze bar was placed in Dolly's now uplifted arms, Colonel Cody's voiced reached a crescendo, a deafening roar came from the onlookers and the balloon was released from its tethers and rose fast and high into the sky.

"Pearl!" Ruby tried to call out, as she saw her friend wrap her arms around Dolly's neck and her legs around her waist. But shock made the words stick tight and hard in Ruby's throat.

Then the fear left her.

Slipped away like dark mud sluiced by clear spring water.

As the balloon soared, Pearl soaring with it, Ruby saw the ribbon tumble from Pearl's braid and flutter towards the ground. Her thick braid quickly unfurled, and her long red hair tumbled free, like a shining red banner.

And Pearl was laughing. Laughing as if the world was a wonderful place, as if amazing things were possible for ordinary girls like her and Ruby. As if she were free.

Watching her friend ascend to the clouds, a smile broke out on Ruby's face that was so broad, her muscles ached.

For Pearl's joy was Ruby's joy, and always would be, from this day on.

If Pearl soared, so would Ruby.

The crowd gave another roar as Dolly dropped

her hands from the trapeze, and for a moment their speed felt too much, too fast, Pearl's hair whipping alarmingly, like a distress call—

And then a great puff of cloth, the parachute it was, opened wide, and gently, gently brought Dolly and Pearl drifting back down to earth, to land with a soft tumble and a multitude of cheers.

As soon as the straps holding Pearl and Dolly were unbound, Pearl ran to Ruby and Ruby ran to Pearl.

Lost in a hug, heart beating against heart, without saying a word both girls knew that their futures were as entangled as *they* were at that moment. . .

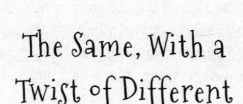

The Same, With a Twist of Different

I can't wait to hug Nana as tightly as Ruby hugged Pearl.

I can't wait to tell her the latest chapter of her story made me cry.

I can't wait to tell her that I just can't wait till the next clue, and the next chapter!

Oh. . .

Having just hurried into the ward, I instantly slow down. Nana's bed is empty, and neatly made up.

"Where is she? What's happened to her?" I splutter, as the four of us stop dead.

"Well, well, well!" I hear a familiar voice call out from the other side of the ward.

Thank goodness...

Nana is over by the window, and in her sky-blue PJs she looks a bit like she's in nurse's scrubs. She even has the footwear; she's not the type to go for comfy slippers, and instead Mum brought in the neon-yellow Crocs Nana had directed her to yesterday.

The one major giveaway that identifies Nana as a patient is – of course – the fact that her arm and fingers are in plaster and in a sling.

"Looking for an escape route, Patsy?" Uncle Dean jokes.

"Just enjoying the view, darling!" Nana says theatrically, sweeping her good arm out towards what I can see is the London skyline. The Shard, the London Eye, the BT Tower ... they're all there, like a postcard image. "AND I'm enjoying being up and about and feeling more like myself!"

That last comment – it's directed at Mum.

Nana's blue eyes zone right in on her, as if she's daring her to even think she's got dementia.

"Anyway, Dean, Scarlet, Zephyr ... let's go and sit down. Have a chat," says Nana.

Mum's jaw clenches.

"Here, Ren, you take this seat," says Dean,

spotting the snub and trying to usher Mum into the seat next to Nana's bed.

Nana sees through the ruse and gingerly perches herself at the end of the bed, the corner facing away from Mum.

"Scarlet, when are you going to turn me into a mermaid like you?" she asks, patting at her pinned-up hair. "Then maybe in the summer holidays, you and I could take a trip to the seaside. Visit Dean and Zephyr in Southend."

"Melbourne, Patsy," Zephyr corrects her with a grin.

"Melbourne, of course! D'oh!" Nana laughs off her mistake. "Get me off these pills! Get me home! And once I'm home I could go online and book the flights. How would you like that, Scarlet? Us two mermaids going off on our own big adventure?"

There's a screech of a chair as Mum gets up and hurries out of the ward.

I start, wondering if I should go after her . . . but then I know Nana is the one who's in here on her own, feeling scared and uncertain about what's going on, and trying to bluster her way through it. Mum is capable and strong and can manage. She's probably out in the corridor now, counting to ten.

"I'm just going to go to the gents' – back in a mo," says Uncle Dean, heading out after Mum instead, which leaves me and Zephyr alone with Nana.

Please, *please* don't let her ask about Mr Spinks or Angie, I suddenly start to fret.

Luckily, my new favourite cousin has plenty of conversation up his sleeve.

"Patsy, I hope it's OK, but Scarlet showed me your story today," he says. "It's really brilliant!"

We were up in my room for ages, Zephyr reading through every chapter so far of *The Pearl in the Attic* as I stared out of the window, hoping but failing to see the wide wings of Angie amongst the grey blur of pigeons swooping and gliding from rooftop to chimney pot.

And then together we read Chapter Six – the best one so far.

"So you shared our little secret, did you, Scarlet?" says Nana, raising her eyebrows at me, though she looks pleased rather than annoyed. "A new player for our little game, eh?"

"Yes!" I say, relieved that she's fine with that, since I don't want her to be cross with me over this, when she's going to be *mega* cross with me pretty soon if

Angie stays away. "And Zephyr worked out your last clue; he guessed that 'rise' was something to do with the bread oven in the bakery."

"Clever boy," Nana beams. "And isn't the old bakery wonderful? When I open my vintage and collectables shop I thought I could use that as a workspace and teach art classes to children!"

I don't dare look at Zephyr and I bet he isn't daring to look at me. Nana probably wouldn't be very impressed to know all her 'vintage and collectables' are currently being crushed into there to free up the flat so it looks presentable to some nosy social worker on Monday.

"I *adored* that last chapter," I say to Nana, to take her mind off the subject of the bakery. "I loved that the girls had had such an adventure, and that Ruby finding a friend in Pearl was this one brilliant thing to happen in a really bleak time."

As soon as I say that, I look shyly at Zephyr, and realize it's kind of the same – with a twist of different – for us. . .

"Oh, I'm *so* glad you both like the story!" says Nana, beaming at us. "It's been really special to me, writing it this last year, ever since. . ."

Nana trails off, blinking.

"Ever since what, Nana?" I ask her, curiosity wriggling in my tummy.

Nana's smile beams full watt again, and she taps her nose.

Aha! She's playing another game with us.

"Can I ask you something, Patsy? Is *The Pearl in the Attic* based on real events?" Zephyr asks, just as intrigued with Nana's writing as I am.

Nana looks at him long and hard, then slowly shakes her head from side to side.

"That, my darlings, is for *me* to know and *you* to find out. You'll need to . . . to kick-start those brain cells!"

Me and Zephyr swap grins across the top of her head, both totally up for our joint challenge.

"Well, for a start," says Zephyr, getting his phone out of his pocket, "I found out the 'Brandt' bakery was for real, and so—"

"Shhh!" says Nana, without looking at the images on the screen. "Boring adults coming! Don't let them find out about our game!"

Ha! She's pointing at Mum and Uncle Dean, who are walking back into the ward.

"Can you at least give us the clue for the next chapter?" I whisper quickly.

Nana fixes me with her sky-blue stare.

"Hmm … I might make you wait a little longer for the next one, my sweetheart," she says, and turns to face the "boring" adults...

"Regular or aloe vera?" asks Zephyr, holding up two types of loo roll on either side of his head.

We're in an aisle of the supermarket with a shopping list Mum gave us, while she's locked away in her tidy white bedroom up in the flat with her computer and spreadsheets and Uncle Dean is off to the nearest storage company, getting cardboard boxes for the next phase of tidying.

I try and muster a smile, but it's hard to come by. It's late Saturday afternoon and Angie still isn't back. We got away with it during our earlier visit to the hospital, but what about this evening? What if Nana asks about Angie then?

"Aw, don't be like that," says Zephyr, dropping his arms. "Don't let me make important life decisions like which loo roll to choose *all* by myself!"

I'm suddenly aware that we're not totally alone. A dark-haired woman, the café owner I met this morning, has stopped beside us.

"Ah, yes, shopping can be a very serious

business," she says, nodding sagely, going along with Zephyr's goofing.

"Oh, hi!" I say, feeling a little awkward and shy. "Um, this is my cousin. Patsy is his grandma too. Zephyr, this is the lady who found Nana. She owns the café at the end of the road."

I don't know what I expect Zephyr to say; a simple hi? A thanks-for-looking-out-for-my-gran? I *don't* expect him to launch into an immediate interrogation.

"So, do you know anything about the history of the shop that Patsy owns?" he asks. He's totally up for Nana's challenge now. He's so determined to find out if the story is based on reality.

"Um, well, no, not really," says the woman, taken aback by Zephyr's lack of small talk. "I mean, it was always a baker's shop, I heard. Just one family owned it since long, long ago. But it's been closed ever since *we've* had our place, and that's more than twelve years now. Why do you want to know?"

"Just interested," says Zephyr, sounding a bit disappointed that his line of enquiry had turned into a dead end so soon.

"I suppose you *could* ask Tom. . ." she says thoughtfully.

"Who's Tom?" I ask.

"Tom Blake; he was the last to run the bakery. He still lived in the flat upstairs, long after he retired," says the café owner. "He sold the place to Patsy, before he moved to the old people's home."

When she says old people's home, she nods, as if it's just along the way.

Which means a piece of the puzzle of *The Pearl in the Attic* might be just along the way too...

And then his phone bleeps and Zephyr's in such a rush to answer it that the loo rolls tumble out of his hands.

"It's a text from Patsy!" Zephyr announces too loudly. "She says, '*Tinkle-inkle-inkle...*'"

The café lady frowns. A guy who's stacking the shelves further along stops to glower our way.

But Zeph and me stare at each other, knowing we've just had the clue to Chapter Seven.

It's just a shame that the bell Nana is referring to is silent just now, with no one – or no *bird* – home to ring it...

The Pearl in the Attic

Chapter 7

Their hair flew free as they ran home, rippling down their backs with every hurried step.

It had been Dolly who tugged the bow that bound Ruby's braid. It had happened before she knew it, as she hugged and congratulated her friend.

"See?" Dolly had said to Colonel Cody, as he looked upon the two girls, arms still around each other, one's hair a thick band of red to her waist, the other's a thick wave of chestnut brown.

"Ah, yes! My, my!" Colonel Cody had remarked, looking upon Ruby and Pearl as if he had been presented with two precious gems.

And then he had said something to the girls that

was quite the most unexpected and extraordinary thing either of them had ever heard...

"Why not?" Pearl breathlessly appealed now to Ruby, holding up Colonel Samuel Cody's calling card as if it were a golden ticket.

She had been badgering Ruby all the way back from the palace.

"Because the colonel did not mean it. Because girls of our age do not go off with strangers. Because it is a crazy scheme. *And* dangerous," said Ruby, as they hurried along Hornsey High Street towards the closed shop and flat above.

At first, when Colonel Cody had presented his card to the girls and asked them to consider joining his touring show as a double act, Ruby's whole chest *ached* at the romance of the idea.

But her head quickly proclaimed that the very notion was impossible, as well as foolhardy.

"You are not a girl to be afraid, Ruby!" Pearl tried to flatter her. "Before the colonel came over to us, didn't you say you would give anything to be up on that trapeze too?"

Ruby had.

But in that same way she might wish she were royalty and that Alexandra Palace was her home.

That she could eat the cakes of Brandt's Baker and Confectioner for breakfast, lunch and dinner every day.

That there were dungeons or at least cellars under Alexandra Palace where her uncle could be locked away and the key mislaid. . .

"And anyway, Ruby, you speak of the danger of going off with Dolly and the troupe," Pearl continued, "but what of the danger of staying here? Living under the same roof as our uncle is as safe as living with a . . . a *wolf*, never knowing when he might turn on anyone within his reach."

"A wolf! Now you're being fanciful," said Ruby, though she could understand the comparison quite well. "Look, we must get you inside the building quickly, so let's talk no more of it."

With that, Ruby lifted her skirts and hastily led the way across the road towards the bakery, before a horse and carriage was upon them.

"But, Ruby," Pearl persisted, even as they stood in the recessed doorway and her dear friend turned the door handle. "How much more thrilling would it be to fly in the air and be paid for the privilege, instead of you working all your days here with Uncle Arthur raging, or me on my hands and knees polishing fire grates before the dawn?"

Ruby's emotions felt raw and tattered.

What Colonel Cody had suggested was a beautiful dream, that they could talk over and whisper of in the attic these next few long months, till Pearl could safely move on.

But it was not reality, Ruby knew.

The reality was, Father had bound her to servitude with her uncle.

The reality was, folk in travelling shows might never see their loved ones and families for years.

The reality was, Aunt Gertrude would never consider it seemly to work in such a profession as theatre.

But Ruby said none of that.

What was most important in her mind was to smuggle Pearl to the safety of the loft, while Uncle Arthur snuffled and snored drunkenly upon the parlour settee, after his Sunday traditions of doing the accounts and spending some of the week's profits in the Three Compasses over the course of the afternoon.

So instead, she simply shushed her friend as they went into the small entrance hall.

"Won't you even think about it, Ruby? They pack up and move on tonight!" Pearl urged her, talking softly over her shoulder as she lightly trod on the first few steps of the staircase.

Ruby, attempting to close the front door as quietly as she could, turned her attention to her friend, and lifted a finger to her lips. But then she looked up and saw what Pearl did not.

A hulking figure turned at the top of the staircase.

His eyes were bloodshot with booze; a slick of alcohol-induced sweat sat about his fat face and thick neck.

He was later back from the public house than expected, and his heaving breath showed that the climb to the apartment above the shop had been a slow, laboured and unsteady one.

"Pearl!" Ruby called out without thinking.

"What *is* this?" Uncle Arthur demanded, swaying slowly. "Why do you dare take this miss back to your lodging, Ruby? And why . . . wait— Pearl, you say? PEARL, you called her? Have I been duped? MADAME! GERTIE!! Get yourself out here, NOW!"

His great girth rocked as he raged, his blurred stare aimed into the apartment.

"Come here and explain yourself at ONCE, woman," he ranted on, "or you'll be feeling a lot *more* than the back of my hand when I get hold of you. And if you end up in the hospital, you'll only have yourself to blame! Gertie! GERTIE! D'you HEAR me?!"

"I hear you," said Aunt Gertrude, appearing in the doorway at the top of the stairs, her face grey, hot spots of pink panic high on her cheekbones.

"Come inside," she said flatly, tight-lipped, holding out a hand to her husband.

Uncle Arthur drunkenly stumbled, grabbing hold of her arm as if his legs might give way, his dopey head swinging low as if he studied his feet and wondered what they might be for.

In that moment, Aunt Gertrude used her free hand to wave to Pearl, trying to signal that she needed to hurry, to get herself to the loft as quickly as possible so Aunt Gertrude could deal with the situation.

Pearl did as she was bid, scurrying as fleet-footedly on the stairs as she was able, hoping, perhaps as they all must, that Uncle Arthur was so soaked in ale that – like so many of his kind – he might collapse in a stupor and wake with no memory of anything that might have passed since several tankards of beer ago.

As for Ruby, her breath was quite gone, her senses frozen at her own stupidity at using Pearl's real name.

She stood at the foot of the stairs, gazing up, wishing what she saw was not happening.

She was only vaguely aware of the draught coming in from the street, the door behind her not closed properly.

She was only vaguely aware of the shy rap of knuckles on the door and the startled "Oh!" of Billy's voice, as he came looking for his wages but found quite an odd scene altogether.

Pearl – petite as she was – was trying to fold herself flatter, to edge around the wobbling largeness of Uncle Arthur before he registered her presence.

"Come inside? COME INSIDE?!" Uncle Arthur suddenly yelled, lifting his head to spit the words in Aunt Gertrude's face. "Who are you to tell me what to do, woman! And how dare you take THIS one into my home, to FOOL me, when I expressly forbade. . ."

Ruby's heart practically pounded out of her chest as she watched her uncle jab his clenched fist into Pearl's collarbone, sending her thudding against the wall.

The force of his blow was hard and cruel, and could have easily broken a bone.

But the force of it too had a very different effect.

As Uncle Arthur pulled his arm back to repeat the punch, his balance quite deserted him.

Quick as Dolly Shepherd's balloon had lifted up, up, *up* from the grass in the grounds of Alexandra Palace, Uncle Arthur fell backwards and tumbled down, down, *down* the flight of stairs, legs, arms and head hitting the walls as he went.

Ruby jumped back, thundering into Billy as her uncle's bear-like body landed in a strangely positioned heap at her feet.

Out of all of them, in the quiet shock of the moment that followed, it was Billy who spoke.

"Oh! You have *killed* him!" Ruby heard him yelp, his hot, frightened breath on her shoulder.

Her eyes fixed on Pearl at the top of the stairs, whose chest heaved with the pain of the blow she had received and the bewilderment of what just happened.

Then Ruby saw her friend clutch her hand to her heart, the hand that still held the calling card of Colonel Samuel Cody.

And Ruby saw in that instant that her and Pearl's minds were as one.

Billy was no enemy of theirs, but no friend either.

His testimony to the police would be that Pearl was the cause of Uncle Arthur's terrible fall.

246

And for a girl to have caused the death of a man . . . it would be the death of *her*.

Ruby stared at Pearl; Pearl stared at Ruby.

And then Ruby turned – shoving the startled boy out of the way – and ran.

A quiet thundering of small boots on the stairs made her glad, knowing that her glance had been understood, and that Pearl was just a few steps behind her.

Pearl caught up with Ruby once she'd crossed the road, darting between carriages, and her hand searched out Ruby's as they ran through the little green surrounded by flower beds at the start of Hornsey High Street.

Pigeons flapped and soared as they hurtled by, hair flying, skirts flapping.

Perhaps one of them was Pearl's pet, who'd flutter and flap around the closed attic window, and wonder why the kind girl and the delicious crumbs were no more. . .

The Story Behind
the Story...

"Here, pass me the ribbon," says Zephyr, holding his hand out.

I lean up off the futon and hand it to him, and then flop back down again.

The untied pages of Chapter Seven are spread out around me. We've read it through twice, totally wowed by what's happened to Ruby and Pearl.

I'm feeling a bit knocked sideways by it, to tell the truth.

"Yeah, that works," says Zephyr, tying the bells he's taken out of Angie's cage to the little catch on the open window in the attic.

He stands back, and we listen to them tinkle gently in the breeze, like a home-made wind chime.

Hopefully, it'll sound like home to Angie.

It's got Mr Spinks's tail wag-wagging, so that's a good sign.

Zephyr came up with the idea of the bell at the window when we were scrabbling inside and outside Angie's giant cage for the latest instalment in *The Pearl in the Attic*. (It was tucked between two boxes of bird food.)

And now we can't wait to get the next clue.

We *have* to read Chapter Eight, and find out what's become of the girls. Did they get away? Or were they caught? Was Pearl tried for their uncle's murder, with Ruby charged too, as an accessory to the crime...?

My phone vibrates.

"Is it Patsy?" asks Zephyr.

"Yep!" I say excitedly, glad she's texting me direct now that we've got each other's numbers.

"What's she saying?" he asks. "Tell her I'm kick-starting my brain cells and ready for action!"

My face falls, my heart sinks, when I see what comes next.

"'*Maybe there IS no Chapter Eight, sweetheart...* Love, Nana xx'," I read aloud. "What does she mean by that?"

Zephyr looks like he's going to speak, then stops and frowns, only for his face to instantly light up again.

"Is Patsy testing us? Teasing us a bit?" he suggests. "I bet when we go in this evening, she'll give us something else!"

"Yeah, but what do we do till then?" I say flatly.

Mum's gone out to find a local print shop to get something crucial and last minute made up for her conference. Uncle Dean was complaining about a sore back after moving all the boxes and is now lounging in the bath with the radio and one escapee yellow duck for company.

Me and Zephyr could get on with moving more stuff, but Mum and Uncle Dean probably have a system.

Also, we don't particularly want to do it.

"Let's go visiting. . ." says Zephyr with a grin.

There's a whole board of buzzers, but none of them has a name beside it.

"What are we meant to do? Press them all?" I say, feeling stumped.

The old people's home was easy to find – the café lady gave us directions earlier.

Mr Spinks is with us. He had his nose to the ground practically all the way here, as if he was doing an impression of a search-and-rescue dog.

But his expert nose isn't much use at sniffing out which buzzer will lead us to the right person. This stocky modern block looks like it's split into individual small flats, and who knows which one we need to get to.

"Well, we could just randomly press a buzzer," Zephyr suggests. "If it's not him, we'll just ask whoever answers which number Tom Blake lives at."

"Or *I* could just tell you, but I'd need to know *why* you want to know," says a deep voice behind us.

We turn to see a balding man who's maybe about the same age as Mum and Uncle Dean, holding a bag of groceries and with a newspaper tucked under one arm. He's scowling, probably thinking we're trouble – two teenagers coming to harass the folk who live here.

"Our grandmother is Patsy Jones. She bought the bakers' shop on the high street from Mr Blake a year ago," says Zephyr, and I'm suddenly so glad of that forthright Australian way he has, instead of my English shyness. "We'd both really like to know more about the history of the place."

The bald man narrows his eyes at us, maybe thinking it's a ruse to wheedle our way in, or maybe wondering why two teenagers are more interested in social history than hanging out in the nearest McDonald's or playing Mario Kart.

Then his face softens, and he begins to nod.

"OK, I'll take you up. He'd enjoy talking about that..."

And so five minutes later, we find ourselves sitting round a small, square dining table, eating Hobnobs with a very frail but lovely man who's clearly in his eighties, and looking at his family photos.

At first, they're relatively recent and not too exciting; there's a photo of Tom from a few decades ago, wearing a straw boater and striped baker's apron and holding his chubby-cheeked grandson – who grew up to be the bald man who let us in downstairs.

But as Tom slides more photos out of the folder, it gets interesting.

"That's like the photo you found online!" I say to Zephyr.

"Ah," says Tom. "Good one, this. About 1947, I think it was taken. See the three boys? The oldest is me, the twins are my brothers. And there's my dad, Joe, and my mum, Agnes. They took over the running of the bakery from my grandad Will and grandma Mary when they retired. That's them."

I stare closely at the various faces. Like the names Tom mentions, nothing really clicks. There's no Ruby, no Pearl, no connection to Nana's story here.

"Who's the old lady who's leaning on you?" Zephyr asks Tom. "She looks a bit stern!"

Tom laughs.

"She might have looked stern on the outside," the old gentleman smiles warmly, "but she was a complete softie, was Auntie Gertrude. She wasn't my *real* auntie; she ran the business with my grandad Will. She just became part of our family, since she had no one of her own."

"We've read about her!" I blurt out. "Our grandmother wrote a story about her and the shop and her husband."

"Ah, yes; the dreadful Arthur, wasn't it? After he died, Gertrude gave my grandad Will the opportunity to train up as a baker and work alongside her. He'd started out as the delivery boy, but he saw his chance and did good!"

"Your grandfather was *Billy*?" asks Zephyr, clicking puzzle pieces together too. "'Cause he's in the story as well!"

"Sorry, *what* story is this?" asks Tom's grandson.

"My nana wrote this whole story about two girls who lived at the shop in 1904," I tell him. "But we didn't know if it was just fiction, or based on truth. She wouldn't say."

"Oh, you mean Ruby and Pearl?" says the grandson. "How did your nana know about them?"

Tom slaps his veined hand against his forehead.

"I lent your nana – Patsy, is it? – a long letter that Ruby wrote Auntie Gertrude about twenty years after they'd seen each other," he says. "In it, Ruby described how she'd felt when she first came to live at the shop, and the events that took place after. I thought Patsy would find it interesting, since it was part of the history of the building. She promised to give it back to me after she read it, but I've just remembered she never did."

So Nana used Ruby's letter as the basis of *The*

Pearl in the Attic. Where's the original letter now in her rabbit warren of a house, I wonder? We have to return it to Tom...

"Was Ruby writing from jail?" Zephyr asks.

"Jail, good lord, no!" exclaims Tom. "What makes you think that?"

"I just thought Pearl and Ruby might've been caught, and charged with Arthur's murder," says my cousin.

"Oh, Arthur didn't *die*," says Tom's grandson. "Not then, anyway! He was a bit bashed up from the fall, but he went on to live another ... how long was it, Grandpa?"

"Enough to make Auntie Gertrude's life hell for a bit longer!" Tom confirms. "Think it was the following winter that he died of influenza. Good riddance. Though my grandad Will – Billy as you know him – felt guilty all his life. He shouted 'You've killed him!', you see, as he was so shocked. And that frightened the poor girls off. They never saw their family again, never knew that they were quite innocent of any wrongdoing..."

"Really?" I gasp. "But what about the letter Ruby sent to Gertrude? Didn't Ruby explain what had happened to them? Didn't Gertrude write back?"

"Ruby didn't leave a forwarding address – she might have thought it was still unsafe to say where they were. She only wrote that she and Pearl had gone and joined this touring show—"

"Colonel Cody's," I interrupt Tom. "That's as far as Nana's version of the story goes at the moment."

"Ah, yes, well, that's as much of the letter as I managed to save," says Tom. "My brothers were mucking around and dropped the lot in a puddle in the yard. Auntie Gertrude was awfully good about it, considering. And she told me the last couple of pages just talked about how Ruby and Pearl had toured with several different companies after Cody's, and how they retired the act and were now quite settled somewhere, running their own little business. I think Ruby just hoped the letter would reach Auntie Gertrude and reassure her that they were both fine."

"That's so nice to know," I say. "But a bit sad too…"

"I think they did all right, though," Tom's grandson says cheerfully. "I mean, we can't prove that it's definitely them, but when I came across this poster online, I had a feeling it was Ruby and Pearl. What do you think?"

Me and Zephyr turn where the bald man is pointing. Above a cabinet filled with ornaments is a large, old-fashioned poster in a clip frame. The writing's in French, which I'm even worse at than Spanish.

But even *I* can understand the flowery headline that reads *Voila! Le GEM GIRLS!*

Below the wording is a drawing of two long-haired young women, smiling at each other as they hang by a trapeze attached to a balloon, a balloon that floats high above a crowd of people that are so small they're dots.

"Ruby and Pearl; it makes total sense that they called themselves The Gem Girls!" I say, getting up for a closer look.

Zephyr's already on his feet too, frowning at the poster. "It sounds sort of like I should know that somehow. . ." he's muttering to himself.

"Do you mind if I take a photo of this?" I remember my manners and ask Tom.

His "Of course!" is drowned out by the sudden ringtone of my phone.

I frown; it's Mum. She's not my favourite person just now, so I almost don't take the call.

And then I wonder if she's got good news; has

Angie heard the tinkle of her bell and come back home?

I mouth "sorry" at Tom and his grandson and quickly take the call.

And guess what; it's not good news.

It's just about the worst news I can imagine.

"Scarlet? Oh, darling; Nana's gone missing. . ."

The Wait-and-See Game

The deal is, Mum and Uncle Dean have gone down to the hospital to find out what on earth has happened, while me and Zephyr are to wait in the flat, in case of . . . I don't know.

I mean, maybe Mum and Uncle Dean are hoping that Nana's going to wander in here, shouting "Yoo hoo! Get the kettle on!"

But the hospital is a long, long walk away along busy roads. *Someone* would have noticed her, wouldn't they? An older lady with glinting hair clips.

It's been over an hour now, and nobody has a clue where she's gone.

One minute, she was asking the nice nurse if she

could change the water in her vase of sunflowers for her; the next, she had vanished.

Padded straight out of the hospital in her bright yellow Crocs and PJs.

At least everyone presumes she's not in the hospital; calls have pinged around every department. Every loo has been checked. She's not in the café sipping tea, and she's not browsing magazines in the hospital shop.

They do have CCTV cameras around the place, so that's the next step, Mum says, but it could take a little while to access the footage. (She's sounding so tense I can just imagine her clenched jaw from here.)

In the meantime, we're just supposed to play the wait-and-see game.

"Where's Mr Spinks?" I ask Zephyr, who's on his dad's laptop, zooming in and out of a street map of the area around the hospital.

"Don't know," he says, his blond eyebrows knitted together in a frown as he stares at the screen.

I feel like I need to find him. And since Nana's flat is a lot neater than it was when we first arrived nearly two days ago, it shouldn't be that hard.

I call out his name, and am rewarded with a little whimper from Nana's bedroom-cum-art-studio. Walking in, I see Mr Spinks curled up on Nana's bed, his head on his paws, looking miserable. He knows something bad has happened. He's sensed our gloom and worry like it's a mist drifting through the flat.

I sit down beside him and stroke his head.

"I don't understand," I admit to him. "Why would Nana disappear? Is she so worried about Mum trying to get her diagnosed with dementia? Maybe she thinks she'll be taken away from all her things?"

I push myself up off the bed, and go to take a look at some of those things. Nana's bedroom is the one room Mum and Uncle Dean haven't touched, since it's full of something personal and special – Nana's artwork.

And all she's been drawing and painting are these circular images. Versions of the balloon, the pearl and the Rose Window canvases that are hanging in the living room. Smaller half-finished canvases are propped up against the walls.

And here on the big desk are scattered loose pages that are the same images but done in dreamy watercolours, pencil sketches, scratchy black pen work. . .

"Mr Spinks," I say, an idea coming to my head. "Walkies!"

Zephyr wanted to come, but what if Nana *did* turn up at the flat? Someone had to stay.

Still, he was *almost* by my side. . .

"Where are you now?" he asks in my ear.

"Going up a very, very steep hill," I say into the phone, panting for breath, but that's partly because me and Mr Spinks ran all the way to Ally Pally, and not just 'cause of the incline.

"Getting closer to the palace?" he asks.

"It's right up ahead," I tell him, gazing up at the building in awe, the stained glass of the great Rose Window glowing blue and red in the sunlight.

"Why don't you let Mr Spinks off the lead and see if he can find her?" Zephyr suggests.

"Because I'm too good at losing Nana's pets," I tell him. "Anyway, I'm nearly at the terrace. I've just got to get across a road and go up a flight of steps and I should be. . ."

"Should be. . . ?" Zephyr repeats.

But the swoop and glide of a particular bird has

caught my eye. Anyone else, not looking too closely, might think it's just a particularly large pigeon, but of course, it's not.

"I think it's Angie!" I say, hurrying now that I see the bird coming in to land along the terrace wall.

"Do the whistle, the one to get her in her cage!" Zephyr urges me, as I look first one way, then another, checking for traffic on the road directly in front of the palace.

"WHEEEEEEEP!" I try, and sure enough the bird turns, wobbling from one foot to another, looking down at me and Mr Spinks with curiosity.

"Well, well, well!" I hear her caw.

"I heard that!" I hear Zephyr say in my ear.

Mr Spinks hears it too, and – for the second time today – pulls so hard that the lead slips right out of my hand, and he hurtles up the set of steps.

"Call you back!" I yell at Zephyr, though I think I may have pressed the off button before he heard that.

I take the steps two at a time, and before I reach the top, I see her.

Nana's on a bench to the left of me, smiling at the sight of Angie, as if she's never seen anything so comical. Then she gives a delighted "Oh!" as Mr Spinks jumps up at her.

"Nana?" I call out.

"Hello, Sita, sweetheart!" she says cheerfully. "Have you finished your shift at the hospital?"

My heart sinks as I sit down beside her.

"Nana, I'm Scarlet..." I say softly, noticing that Nana's curls are coming unpinned, unfurling, glinting clips coming undone.

"More lilac, I'd say," says Nana, nodding at my hair and smiling as if she's made the best joke. "So, is this your doggy?"

"No, it yours – it's Mr Spinks!" I tell her.

"Oh, no, sweetheart, Mr Spinks is next door's cat. He always comes under the gap in the fence. Don't you remember?"

OK, so now I suddenly *do* remember that it was the name of next door's cat back at Nana's old house in Southend, the one in the bent photo Zephyr gave me last night. Nana must have named her Staffie after him, then. But why is she talking as if—

"Ha! Whoo! What on earth kind of bird is this, do you think?" she asks in delight, as Angie flutters on to the arm of the bench beside her.

"It's a parrot, Nana," I tell her, wriggling my arms out of my hoodie. I'll need it to bundle around Angie so I can keep her safe and get her home.

"Oh, aren't you clever?" says Nana, leaning back as I lunge for Angie and successfully catch her.

The parrot struggles a little as I tuck her under my arm, but when I pull the hood of my top over her eyes, she seems to settle.

"What will you do with it?" Nana asks.

"Well, take it back to your flat," I say, feeling the tears start to prickle in my eyes. I'm a bit scared about what this means.

"Do you know where that is, dear? I can't quite remember. And I'm getting a bit cold now. . ."

Nana looks down at her feet. Her yellow Crocs are muddy.

"Did you come along the walk where the old railway line used to be?" I ask her. It's how I guessed Nana might get here. She'd talked about the walk starting not too far from the hospital, and how it took you – as a shortcut, I suppose – straight into Ally Pally Park.

"Yes, I did! Clever you! It's such a pretty walk. I must take Manny sometime. He'd love it. . ."

You know, I have never been so glad to see my mum as I am now. She's walking along the terrace from a different direction than the one I took. She's smiling at me, hurrying, holding a fleecy blanket she keeps in the car.

"Hello, Mum!" she says to Nana, sounding bright and perky, even though she must be jelly inside. Mum in Practical Mode, one hundred per cent.

"Hello, Renuka!" says Nana, looking delighted to see her. "Is Daddy with you?"

"No," says Mum, still smiling, but with a little choking sound in her voice. "Here, let's get this around you. The sun's out, but there's quite a breeze up here, isn't there?"

"Oh, but you don't feel it when you're in love!" laughs Nana, standing up and taking a few steps towards the stone balustrade of the terrace.

She stands there looking out over the trees and the grass to the rooftops of Hornsey down below and the high-rise tips of central London in the distance, swaying gently while she hums a tuneless song.

"I'm sorry," I say quietly to Mum as I start to cry. "I didn't want to believe it was true."

"I'm sorry too," says Mum, sliding over to put her arm around me as we watch Nana, lost in her strange but happy bubble. "And I didn't want it to be true either. But well done for finding her, Scarlet."

"*And* I found Angie," I say, managing a snotty smile, as I show Mum the softly moving bundle under my arm. "But how did you know I was coming to look for Nana here?"

"Zephyr was emailing his dad while he was on the phone to you. When Dean told me, I drove straight up here. Dean is in his car and should be here soon too."

And in this bizarre, sad and odd moment, I think I want to ask her something.

"Mum . . . what did you and Nana fight about that day when she was moving?" I ask.

"She said – she said some pretty upsetting things to me, darling," Mum says softly. "But I've been reading up about dementia, and it can make you insensitive to other people's feelings. So perhaps it was starting even back then. Or maybe she was just being her usual, difficult self! Ha!"

"Nana is difficult?" I frown. I've only ever seen her as funny and bright and wonderful.

"It was very hard, growing up just me and Nana, Scarlet. It was always *her* way or no way. She always seemed very disappointed in me for being . . . ordinary. For not liking adventure. And she told me in no uncertain terms that day what a fool she's thought I'd been over the years, letting things slip through my fingers."

"Like my dad?" I ask.

Mum looks at me sharply, but we don't say any more about it, because Uncle Dean is hurrying towards us, Nana has started to sing at the top of her voice, and Mr Spinks is keeping her company with a yodelling sort of howl.

"You have GOT to be joking!" says Mum, but she is laughing, tilting her head back and laughing, till I can't help laughing too, at the strange new version of our useless little family. . .

Family #notsofail

Melbourne, Australia, 2017

"I thought Australia was meant to be hot," I moan, fastening the buttons on the pink tweed jacket I stole from Nana's clothes rack all those weeks ago.

"Quiet!" Zephyr orders me. "If you come to visit us in Melbourne in the summer holidays, you get our winter. Deal with it. And Missy's the only one supposed to moan in this family!"

Well, that's not exactly true. Nana's been moaning a bit, wondering how much longer it's going to take to get to this "special" café that Zephyr wants us to see.

Great-Aunt Sita has already moaned about the distance, even though Uncle Dean was pushing her in her wheelchair. My aunt Angie – Zephyr's mum –

just rolled her eyes good-naturedly and steered Sita off to have a coffee overlooking the ocean, while the rest of us mosey a bit further into town.

"Come on, Nana Patsy!" Missy insists, slipping her small hand into Nana's. Her other hand is held by her granny Kate, the widow of Manny. I worried that they might get a bit prickly with each other, being first wife and second wife and everything, but Nana and Kate have been getting on like a house on fire, laughing at all the annoying things "their" Manny used to do.

"So what's so special about this 'special' café?" I ask my cousin. Zephyr's been very mysterious about it, ever since we arrived a couple of days ago.

I think Mum and Dean are both in on the secret; they keep swapping matching sibling grins at each other.

"Well," says Zephyr, "remember when we went to visit Tom at the old folks' home, and saw his Gem Girls poster, and I thought it looked kind of familiar?"

"Yeah, I think so," I say, trying to remember the details of that crazy day.

The day I faced up to the fact that my beloved nana really did have dementia. (And also wasn't as perfect as I thought she was, same as Mum isn't as annoying as I thought she was. . .)

The whole shock of the dementia diagnosis being true: it felt huge and awful and upsettingly weird at first, but it's now sort of OK, sort of normal.

Especially since Nana's just in the early stages. She hadn't been eating or looking after herself properly before her fall, so it had worsened a bit. But now she's on medication that keeps her pretty level, and she has a carer who pops in to check on her, plus all the lovely locals in her street to keep an eye on her too.

"Well, *this* is why it felt like I recognized the name," says Zephyr.

He points to a cute café with mismatching pastel-painted tables and chairs outside. The name of it is painted in this swirly art deco style.

The Gem Girls Café.

"What is this?" I ask, uncertain what I'm seeing.

"This version of the café has only been open a couple of years," says Dean as he ushers Nana and Kate to sit at one of the outdoor tables. "But the new owners named it after the original Gem Girls tea shop, which was on this site for decades."

"Check it out!" says Zephyr, passing me a menu,

and making sure Nana has one too. "Ruby and Pearl!"

The cover of the menu is a patchwork of photos from all different eras. The only thing that's the same is the name of the shop in them all, and the two women pictured in their pretty aprons, one in glasses and one without. In some of the pictures they look in their late twenties, and then they get progressively older, their hairstyles gradually changing, till they're women in their sixties, still in pretty aprons, still smiling.

"Really?" says Nana. "*This* is the real Ruby and Pearl?"

"The real deal!" says Zephyr. "Look, there's even a bit about them on the back of the menu..."

A panel of information sits to the left of a black-and-white photo of two girls, hanging from the trapeze of a hot air balloon. I scan the info.

"So they performed in a park in Melbourne in 1928, and their parachute didn't open fully?" I read.

"Pearl broke her leg really badly," says Zephyr, too impatient to let me read on. "So she and Ruby decided that was that; they'd give up performing. And Melbourne seemed as good a place to settle as anywhere. They started running a tea shop, selling cakes like the ones back in Gertrude's bakery."

I look around, and get it. I feel quite at home here already. Same as I feel at home in North London. You never know, I might even feel at home in Ecuador one of these days. Mum and me; we've talked about her maybe contacting my dad sometime in the future. She's done a little digging and found out he's still there, married to a local woman, and has two kids. So maybe that's another part of my slowly extending family that I'll get to know eventually, but I'd better work harder in Miss Kendrick's Spanish class in the meantime. ("*Hola, Papá,*" won't get me too far. . .)

"This – this is pretty cool," I say, nodding down at the actual, animated faces of Ruby and Pearl and feeling prickles on my arms, even though the Australian winter's day isn't exactly freezing.

"And you want to know something else that's pretty cool?" asks Mum as she settles down beside Nana and takes her hand in hers.

"Go on," I say, wondering what's coming next. Nana's in on *this* secret, I can tell, since she's beaming so much. She's looking beautiful today, in her denim jacket and with her mermaid blue hair twinkling with jewelled clips.

"We all know Nana's doing great at the moment, but she *is* going to need more help down the line," says Mum. "So she and I were thinking, Scarlet, how about you and me sell up our place in Chelmsford and move in with Nana, in the Hornsey flat?"

"What do you think, Scarlet?" asks Nana. "A little adventure for us all?"

"I – I . . . yes! Yes, please!" I splutter, smiling at her, smiling at Mum. We've been staying at Nana's most weekends since her fall, and it's come to feel more like home than anywhere else, especially with Mr Spinks and Angie around. "But won't that be a long commute for your job, Mum?"

"What, that job I *hate*?" Mum laughs. "Well, I've been mulling something over, Scarlet... I was thinking that maybe I should hand my notice in, and turn the old bakery downstairs into a café? You know, all vintage teacups and Nana's artwork and quirky stuff around the place..."

My heart skips a beat. The last couple of months, Mum's done a great job of sorting and selling off lots of Nana's hoarding mountain on eBay. But she's been whittling it down to the good stuff, and I can totally see how that would work in a cute, retro café.

"We can learn to make all those Victorian and

Edwardian-style cakes, Scarlet," Nana says, her eyes shining. "That could be our speciality. Do you remember? Langue de chats cones, genoises, tarts with damson jam and fondant roses..."

"I do," I say. I have all of Nana's story in a folder in my room at her flat. We still haven't found the original letter she based it on, but it'll turn up, tucked away safely in some random place, like so many things. Only last week, I came across her original wedding certificate inside the DVD case of *Titanic*, when we sat down to watch it on Saturday afternoon together.

And then something hits me as I sit here at the Gem Girls café, with Ruby and Pearl's faces smiling up at me. Now that we're going to be living with her, Nana and I can work on the rest of their story, especially now we've found out *this* amazing part of it ... and maybe me and Zephyr can do more internet research on them too?

"So, how about we call our little café in Hornsey after the Gem Girls?" Mum suggests, her face lit up with excitement at the thought of her new venture. "What do you think, Scarlet?"

"Maybe I have a better idea," I say.

I'm thinking of the story that obsessed Nana

since she moved to Hornsey, her beautiful paintings, the room I sleep in when we stay, where I sometimes lie in the dark and imagine I can almost hear the distant chat and giggles of two girls...

There is only one name it can be, isn't there?

"We should call it The Pearl in the Attic..."

Whoops and yeses break out at the two tables we're all crushed around: me, Mum and Nana, Dean and his mum Kate, Zephyr and Missy. My family.

Then of course there's Aussie Aunt Angie, and Angie back home, Great-Aunt Sita who I'm named after and Mr Spinks who I'm not. Ha!

Families are funny, fragmented things, aren't they?

Look at Ruby and Pearl, who went on to make their own, here in this sunny city by the sea. And now I've found *my* jumble of mismatching sorts of relatives.

It's like that nurse said, back in Nana's ward when she was poorly: someone really *does* need to invent a new batch of names to describe everyone we love.

And in the meantime, I need to order some cake...

Epilogue

Melbourne, 1954

Ruby placed a little fan of apple slices and a tiny pot of honey beside the pancakes on both the plates, then stood back to admire her handiwork.

Making food pretty: it was a habit she couldn't get out of, even though she and Pearl had finally sold the café and retired a few months back.

"Here we are!" she called out to Pearl as she walked through the French doors that took her out on to the veranda of the old wooden house.

Pearl looked up from the morning paper and smiled in delight.

Her hair was still long, but faded to a pale strawberry blonde that was streaked with white. She wore it bundled up loosely, with a mauve chiffon scarf tied around her head. Ruby's dark hair was steely grey, but she'd long ago cut it short, and wore it wavy, with kiss curls at both temples, copied from her favourite Hollywood movie stars.

It's what the customers of the Gem Girls café had loved; not just the food and the fabulous cakes, but the two wonderful women who ran the place for nearly forty years, full of character and warmth. They'd become quite the institution in the neighbourhood, children coming for years who'd take their *own* children in turn to meet the remarkable Miss Ruby and Miss Pearl. . .

"Did you know," the mums and dads would say to their little ones, "that Miss Ruby and Miss Pearl were once upon a time quite famous? That they hung on to a hot air balloon that took them high into the sky, then floated down on silk parachutes?"

The children would smile, but were never that impressed. And why would they be? So many wonders they quite took for granted now. Amelia Earhart and Amy Johnson and all those other aviatrixes had long since flown over oceans and continents single-handedly. Nowadays, it was even possible for ordinary, if rich, people to fly all the way from Sydney to London in just a few days, with stop-offs in fascinating countries, instead of the weeks-long journey by boat that had taken Ruby and Pearl and the show company to Australia all those years ago. There was even talk that one day in the not too distant future there'd be rockets built that could take you into space. The Americans and Russians were working on it already, Ruby had read in the paper. . .

Before she placed the plates down on the little table, Ruby drank in the view over rooftops and trees of the morning sun glinting on the sea. For nearly forty years they'd run the Gem Girls café, and they'd loved every tiring, busy minute of it. But to slow down and have this view to enjoy was really wonderful.

Now and again, when the crickets stilled, the golden light transported Ruby back to the days when she was a child, standing looking over the wafting, waving cornfields of Kent.

"Look at this!" said Pearl, holding up the paper for Ruby to see as she sat down. "There's been a new world record set in running; an Englishman called Roger Bannister has run a mile in under four minutes!"

Ruby picked her specs up off the table and read the story.

"What an achievement!" she remarked. "What's the date? It'll surely go down in history. . ."

Both woman glanced up at the top of the newspaper, and then grew quiet.

They were both thinking the same thing, remembering the most wonderful day that had turned into the most terrible, and changed the course of their lives.

"Fifty years ago to the day. . ." Ruby said finally. "Can you believe it?"

"Seems like forever ago," murmured Pearl, smiling sadly, though her cheeks still dimpled.

"Yes, it does," Ruby agreed, taking her glasses off again, and thinking of Aunt Gertrude, who'd been so kind in her own way. Ruby always hoped life had turned out well for her in the end. She'd have loved to know; had even sent Aunt Gertrude a letter once (without letting her know where she and Pearl now were) and she hoped she got it. Ruby had never told Pearl she sent it; Pearl still, even to this day, occasionally had nightmares about being hunted down and caught.

"Well, look at us now," Ruby said cheerily. "We've not done too badly, have we?"

"No. No, we haven't," said Pearl, her smile brightening as Ruby reached out to her.

The two women sat hand in hand, staring out the horizon, where the blue sky met the blue ocean, both lost in memories of a *different* sky they saw from an attic window a whole lifetime ago. . .

Also by Karen McCombie:

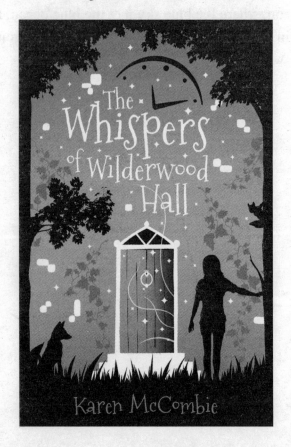

The Whispers of Wilderwood Hall

Karen McCombie

After leaving her friends to move to a crumbling Scottish mansion, Ellis is overcome by anxiety and loneliness. Then she hears whispers in the walls … and finds herself whisked back in time to 1912.